ON THE TRACK . . .

As she reached the trees a harsh chattering, startlingly loud in the quiet of the morning, halted her. The monkeys again! Karen had forgotten them. She went forward more slowly and as soundlessly as she could. Where were the monkeys? Had she disturbed them—or was her quarry still about? She slipped cautiously round a huge gum tree, its trunk showing smooth and bare through the rags of red bark. And stopped dead in her tracks.

Facing her in the fork of a tree only ten yards away crouched a leopard. . . .

KAREN'S LEOPARD
was originally published by
Henry Z. Walck, Inc.

Critics' Corner:

About the Author and Illustrator:

BETTY DINNEEN was born and educated in England. From 1958 to 1964 she lived in Nairobi, Kenya, and then she and her family moved to California. Mrs. Dinneen writes: "My book grew out of my nostalgia for Kenya. When I first settled in America I was very homesick for Africa. I wrote about what I knew best, the daily life with its fascinating contacts with a different race of people and the animal world which never ceased to be a source of excitement and wonder to me. Karen's leopard really did leave its paw marks under my bedroom window. The bees did nest in my roof. That's Africa for you."

CHARLES ROBINSON has illustrated more than thirty-five children's books and in 1971 was awarded a Gold Medal by the Society of Illustrators. He and his wife, who is a teacher, live in New Jersey with their three children.

Karen's Leopard
(Original title: *A Lurk of Leopards*)

BETTY DINNEEN

illustrated by Charles Robinson

AN ARCHWAY PAPERBACK
POCKET BOOKS • NEW YORK

Author's Note

Nairobi dwellers will know that I have juggled with the geography of the Langata and Karen districts, erecting an escarpment where none exists and shifting the game park to suit my convenience. I have also peopled the neighborhood with characters who are figments of my imagination, and do not in any way represent past or present residents of Nairobi.

KAREN'S LEOPARD

Henry Z. Walck edition published 1972

Archway Paperback edition published January, 1975

L

Published by
POCKET BOOKS, a division of Simon & Schuster, Inc.,
630 Fifth Avenue, New York, N.Y.

Archway Paperback editions are distributed in the U.S. by Simon & Schuster, Inc., 630 Fifth Avenue, New York, N.Y. 10020, and in Canada by Simon & Schuster of Canada, Ltd., Markham, Ontario, Canada.

Standard Book Number: 671-29712-0.
Library of Congress Catalog Card Number: 72-3205.
This Archway Paperback edition is published by arrangement with Henry Z. Walck, Inc. Copyright, ©, 1972, by Betty Dinneen. All rights reserved. *Karen's Leopard* was originally published under the title: *A Lurk of Leopards*.
This book, or portions thereof, may not be reproduced by any means without the permission of the original publisher: Henry Z. Walck, Inc., 19 Union Square W., New York, New York 10003.

Printed in the U.S.A.

This book is dedicated to my children, Penny and Hugh, who are African by birth, British by descent and American by upbringing. An interesting mixture.

Contents

1

Karen's Wish

"I wish I had a wild pet," said Karen Elliott. "Something fierce and furry. Like a lion cub. Mmm, yes, a lion cub would be smashing. Or a baby cheetah, all legs and ears. Richard? Hey, Richard, are you listening?" She rolled over on her back, blinked up at the sizzling African sun overhead, then turned to stare at her companion with sun-dazzled eyes.

Richard Faulkner was watching a chameleon. It clung to the spine of a brown-covered book lying on the grass in front of him. "Hmmm? Yes, I'm listening," he said absently.

"When I first came to live in Kenya," went on Karen, "I thought everyone would have that sort of pet." She plucked a blade of grass and sucked it thoughtfully. Further down the lawn the sprinklers hissed rhythmically as they spun their watery webs over the lawn outside Richard's house. It was a very hot day.

"You've got the dogs," said Richard. "Eight of 'em, counting the pups." He poked the chameleon very gently and it took a step and stopped, one leg raised, one many-faceted eye aimed at Richard, the other looking straight ahead. "And once you had a mole rat, but you let it go. And that tree hyrax with the broken leg, that died, didn't it? And what about your hunting spider?"

"Poof," said Karen. She tickled the chameleon with her blade of glass. "Put him on the lawn, Richard, and let's see him change color."

The chameleon, dislodged from the book, took a slow step, rocked, and froze like a gundog scenting a pheasant. Its long sticky tongue flickered out and in, and a small black beetle disappeared as if by magic from its perch on a clover leaf. The chameleon swallowed.

"Bulls-eye," said Richard.

"Did you ever raise a lion cub?" asked Karen. "I mean, did your father? I know you've had impala and bushbuck and things."

"Nope," said Richard. "One of the game wardens is keen on lions. Dad gets the small fry."

Karen sighed. Richard's father was an honorary game warden. On weekends and in his spare time he helped with the work at the Nairobi Game Park, which was only a few miles away from where Richard and Karen lived. Often he had orphaned or injured animals to care for. "Girls are never game wardens, are they?" she asked, but she knew the answer already.

"Nope," said Richard.

"I wish I were Joy Adamson," said Karen dreamily. "With a pet like Elsa."

"Yes, and look at all the *shauris* they had with Elsa. Use your loaf, Karen. What would you do with it when it grew up? It would cost a small fortune to feed. Plenty of people do rear cubs, of course, but they nearly always end up in a zoo. They aren't afraid of people, see? So, even if they can fend for themselves, it isn't safe to turn 'em loose."

"You're so practical," said Karen, deep in gloom. She rolled back onto her stomach and buried her face in the cool shadowy grass beneath a pepper tree. "I—wish—I—had—a—fierce—and—furry—pet," she whispered to the hard African earth.

Karen was twelve but small for her age. Young for her age, too, so her mother said. She had long fair hair, streaked by the sun and twisted up into a careless pony tail. Her eyes were blue and her nose resembled a blob of putty, a freckled blob of putty at that. She wore faded jeans and an old checked shirt with the sleeves rolled up above her elbows. She was as thin as a knitting needle and she bit her fingernails. And her mind ran on animals.

"Richard?" she began again. But Richard was intent on the chameleon. "Look, he's changing color," said Richard.

The chameleon, once a sad brown like the book

cover, was now a dismal yellowish-green. Richard looked proud.

Karen yawned. She was tired of watching.

"Let's go over to my house and visit the pups," she said. "Richard? Hey, listen to me. Richard!"

"No peace," said Richard. "OK, mosquito."

He placed the chameleon in a cardboard box which he left at the foot of the pepper tree. Then he hauled Karen to her feet. "Race you," he said.

They raced.

The Elliotts and the Faulkners were next-door neighbors. Each low, stone-built, homemade Kenya house sat on a ten-acre plot some twelve miles outside Nairobi. Richard was Kenya-born. His mother had died when he was a baby, and he lived alone with his father. He was a quiet, solitary boy of fifteen, but he had befriended Karen the previous year when she had come out from England to join her parents. He enjoyed showing her something of the Kenya he dearly loved, and he taught her everything he could about the animals and birds which abounded there, both inside and outside the game park. Karen treated him with a mixture of hero worship and bossiness. She was used to having him at her beck and call.

The quickest way from the Faulkners' garden to the Elliotts' was through the hedge. As Karen struggled through the gap in the sharp-thorned kei apple hedge, a shaggy black dog hurled himself straight at her.

"Ouch! Woops! Down, you lump. Richard? Hey, wait for me. Down, Ajax, you horrible dog," said

4

Karen. She puffed and panted and hugged the dog, dodging the affectionate licks of his tongue.

"He gets bigger and bigger, but he doesn't act any older," said Richard disapprovingly.

"He's a Peter Pan dog. He never grows up." And Karen, getting her second wind, set off again at full speed, hoping to steal a march on Richard. The big black dog, an Alsatian, bounded along at her heels.

Beyond the hedge there was a stretch of rough, sun-yellowed grass. Richard's long legs soon helped him to overtake Karen. He tore over the grass, crossed the drive, and raced on toward the low white house. There was a second hedge, of Kaffir honeysuckle, around the house, enclosing within it a semicircle of smooth green lawn, trees and flower beds.

On the lawn in front of the house, in the shade of a jacaranda tree, was a wire enclosure and a large dog kennel. Outside the enclosure lay a second Alsatian, smaller than the first. Her fur was golden marked with black. Within the enclosure wriggled six fat puppies.

"Tina!" called Karen. The second dog rose and came trotting toward her, pausing to sniff and wag at Richard as he ran, more slowly now, over the last stretch of grass toward the puppies. Karen, flanked on both sides by the dogs, crossed the drive and skipped after Richard.

While Richard flopped down on the lawn, Karen reached into the enclosure and captured a puppy.

"Boofuls," she cooed.

"Urk," said Richard.

"You are boofuls, aren't you?" said Karen to the puppy. "Oh, isn't it awful, just two more weeks and they'll be gone."

"Have you found homes for them all?"

"Most. But I wish a neighbor would buy one so I could watch it grow up. Richard, are you sure you don't want a puppy . . . ?"

"Sure I'm sure," said Richard. "I've told you. Being visited by Ajax is bad enough."

"Oh well," sighed Karen.

Mrs. Elliott came out on the veranda steps with Jenny, Karen's little sister, in her arms. She set the toddler down and gave her a guiding push toward the group on the lawn.

"Karen, take Jenny, will you? The house is full of bees and I'm afraid she'll sit on one."

"Bees bad again?" asked Richard.

Karen nodded, and made encouraging noises to Jenny, very similar to the noises she had made to the puppies. "Yep," she said, after a while. "We had stewed rhubarb for lunch, and that brought them out in force. Joshua was just starting a massacre when I came over to find you. He squashes them with his thumb!" she added in an awed voice.

For some months the Elliotts had been sharing their house with a nest of wild bees. It had happened like this. One afternoon when the Elliotts were enjoying their tea, they were startled by a sudden furious buzzing outside, like the whirring of a giant dentist's drill. The noise came closer and louder, and Karen, poking her nose cautiously out of the French doors, found a cloud of bees harassing the

veranda. The bees settled in a long crawling cluster round a drainpipe, and for the rest of the day the Elliotts went in and out by the back door.

The next day they were relieved to find that the bees were gone from the veranda, but at breakfast Joshua, the Elliotts' African house servant, announced with a broad smile that they had merely retired to the back of the house and had found a way into the roof through a loose tile. Joshua was pleased; he was fond of honey. And there the matter rested. The Elliotts lived in the house, and the bees resided in the roof.

"Well, that's Africa for you," said Karen, hugely delighted.

But as the hot season got into its stride the bees became more and more active. They zoomed bad-temperedly in at the windows, and crawled over the furniture and along the floor. Joshua trod on them with his bare, horny feet. Jenny was rescued a hundred times from an imminent sting.

One night Joshua and two of his cronies tried to smoke out the nest. Karen and her parents, sitting safely indoors, heard excited whisperings and smothered chuckles. They smelled smoke. Then came yelps and a flood of Swahili which Mr. Elliott would not translate for Karen. Joshua came in, crest-fallen, to report. The attempt had been a failure. The bees had not cooperated; they had fought back. They had won.

"Bees are fierce and furry," said Richard now,

looking slyly at Karen out of the corner of his eye. "Couldn't you tame a bee?"

Karen refused to answer. Jenny, however, dimpled at Richard. She had big brown eyes, a fluff of curls, and was at the very feminine age of eighteen months.

Mrs. Elliott reappeared, carrying a shopping basket.

"I'm going to fetch the dog meat. Want to come?" she asked the puppy watchers. "And Karen. Do remind me to get one of those insect bomb things. We simply must get rid of those bees! It's them or me."

"If it would only rain," said Karen, but the sun stared brazenly down at them. The long rains, which come in Kenya approximately from March to May, were overdue. Day after day the heat continued, while gardeners searched the sky daily for omens and prophesied disaster.

Richard directed the traffic as Mrs. Elliott backed her ancient car out from its wisteria-covered shelter. Then Jenny was inserted in the baby seat and Karen and Richard crowded into the back. The dogs watched with wistful expressions and lolling tongues.

"Look, there's Dogo, paying a call on Tina," said Karen, pointing down the drive as they set off. This dog was long-bodied and short-legged; his ears flopped and his rear end wagged with his skinny tail. Ajax gave a gruff bark, and Tina lowered her ears and her eyelashes demurely.

"He admires Tina like anything," said Karen.

"But Ajax doesn't really care. He only pretends to be tough." Ajax had bounded stiff-legged and aggressive toward the newcomer. But when they met, Ajax's beautiful furry tail wagged just as fast as the dachshund's slender one.

Dogo belonged to Mrs. Liversedge, who lived on the other side of Karen. She had only recently returned from a long stay in Europe and the Elliotts were just beginning to know her ways. "But of course it's really Mrs. Liversedge who belongs to Dogo," Karen explained to Richard while the car gathered speed. "The house runs round him. It's Dogo's breakfast, Dogo's walk, Dogo's dinner, all day long!"

"To look at her, you'd think she'd have half a dozen mastiffs, or a pack of foxhounds," said Richard.

Heat mirages shimmered on the dusty road as they headed for the small local shopping center.

"Jeepers," said Karen, as they turned a corner. "More smoke!"

Grass fires were commonplace at the tail end of the hot season. Here a field belonging to a dairy farm was already half blackened as a fire steadily ate its way across the dry yellow grass. A line of men beat at the approaching flames with rough brooms made of wattle twigs. They had the fire well under control. Behind the line of fire dozens of long-legged, white-plumed birds swooped and hovered.

"Hey, Karen, look—storks!"

"So they are—and there's a heron. And another! Whatever are they after?"

"Insects, grasshoppers mainly, that fly up to escape the fire. If they do escape, they get eaten by the storks. If they don't escape, the storks eat them roasted. Very tasty. It's a good life—for the storks."

"I loathe grass fires," said Mrs. Elliott, slowing down as a herd of Boran cattle surged into the road. A small African child clad in a short shirt yelled at them, and drove them back onto the side of the road. "I'm always afraid our field will be next and I'm sure it's dry enough. I do so wish the rains would break." Her garden was her pride and joy.

"Well, that one's nearly out," said Richard, regarding the fire with an expert eye. "But Dad says there've been a rotten lot of grass fires in the game park lately. And some of the animals are calving already and there's no young grass for the *totos*." He shook his head solemnly. "Hey, but just look at those clouds, Karen, piling up over the Ngongs. Thunderheads! They look as if they're going to burst at any moment." The heavy yellow clouds moved queasily over the hills and the sound of thunder came faintly to Karen's ears.

While Mrs. Elliott shopped, Karen kept Jenny amused and called greetings to passing Africans. Many were friends of Joshua or Mungai, the Elliotts' gardener, and she knew them well. Richard walked up to the post office to look for mail. He came back with a bundle of letters and magazines stuffed under his arm and one long airmail envelope which he was studying with interest.

"It's come!" he told Karen, who looked blank. "I've asked two boys from school to stay over the Easter holidays. Angus and Jock Duncan. They're boarding while their parents are on leave in Scotland, and that's no fun. Anyway, this is a letter for Dad from the Duncans. They wouldn't bother to write all this just to say no, would they?" And he weighed the letter in his hand.

"Dunno," said Karen. She frowned a little and chewed at her thumbnail. She had grown accustomed to having Richard to herself during school holidays.

"Oh dear." Mrs. Elliott, laden with parcels, came hurrying back to the car. "Karen, love, do take this horrid drippy dog-meat bundle. They're always so mean with the wrapping paper. Tuck it down on the floor somewhere—it can't hurt this car. The store is quite out of insect bombs. I shall have to get one in town."

The dogs were lined up on the drive to welcome them home. Ajax and Tina leaped up at the doors, their attention caught by the smell of raw and gory meat, but Dogo sat primly on the grass, paws together, his warm admiring gaze fixed on Tina.

Richard carried Jenny piggyback into the house, while Karen helped her mother with the parcels. Joshua did not work on Saturday afternoons, but when they reached the kitchen they found that he had left a long line of bee corpses laid out on the draining board for them to admire. The sun was going down and the day was beginning to cool. The bees were retreating to their nest.

"Thirty-two! Joshua's broken his own record," said Karen, who had been counting the bees. She helped herself to a gingernut from the plateful her mother had begun to arrange.

Mrs. Elliott smacked at Karen's hand. "Stop it, you pigupine. Wait for tea. Richard, will you have tea with us?" Richard grinned and accepted; it was part of the regular Saturday routine. From outside a sudden breeze whipped the gingham curtains out into the room. Mrs. Elliott shivered, and went to close the back door.

"There's a wind getting up. Listen to the leaves rustling in the gum trees. The weather's changing at last," she said. "Karen, don't forget to bring the pups indoors."

"I'll do it now." Karen slid through the door as her mother began to shut it. She paused on the doorstep, looking up at the tall swaying trees with their quivering leaves. A new noise caught her attention. Beyond the trees, crisply outlined against the deep blue sky, two crowned cranes flew, calling their strange wild call as they went. Karen's heart sang as it always did at the sight of these beautiful birds. Happily she went to fetch the puppies.

And later that evening she was awakened from her first warm doze by a fresh sound. A sound at once familiar and yet unusual enough to jerk her up in bed so that she could hear more distinctly. First lightly, then more and more heavily, came the drumming of a million tiny drumsticks on the hollow roof. Rain! The wind prowled round the little house as if seeking a way in, roaring and lashing its tail among the creaking trees. Karen shivered.

"Poor old animals," she muttered. "All that wet fur!"

Back she snuggled into her bed and pulled the blankets closer round her shoulders. Sleepily her mind reached out, seeking the fierce and furry pet which shared her dreams, bringing it in out of the wet and the wind. Patter-patter went the raindrops on the windowpane, and patter-patter went wet furry feet in Karen's dream.

The rainy season had begun at last.

2

On the Prowl

Hour after hour through that April night the rain poured down. And, while human beings stayed snugly indoors or took shelter as fast as they were able, the wild creatures awoke and emerged. The dry cracked earth sucked and swallowed, the trees and plants drank, drank, drank after the long drought. Earth became mud, grassland became swamp, and roadways turned to rivers as Nature turned on all her taps at last.

The young leopardess climbed steadily up the shiny wet boulders and grassy ledges of the escarpment. Her thick silky fur shed the rain effortlessly and though occasionally she paused to shake the raindrops from her whiskers with a catlike shrug, she did not seem hampered by the wet. Her low-slung body, heavy now with cubs, moved easily over rocks and through clefts clotted with shrubs and sodden matted grass. She was hungry. She was hunting.

She came over the lip of the escarpment with one lithe bound and stopped, crouching low, as an alien scent reached her sensitive nose. In front of her stretched a few feet of coarse grass, then a tangle of crooked thorn trees, wattle and bush. At the edge of the trees something moved. The leopardess snarled, a deep coughing snarl. There was a scuffle as the intruders retreated awkwardly, then a weird and dreadful cackling broke out. The leopardess snarled again. She crept forward, belly low, head moving a little, snakelike, from side to side.

The hyenas chuckled their obscene slobbering chuckle. They shifted uneasily, giving way before the leopardess. Then, together, they turned and fled into the bush.

The leopardess advanced to the spot where she had first sensed the hyenas. She raised her head and her nostrils flared. From the tree above her head there came the smell of putrid meat. In that tree, a week before, she had stored the half-eaten carcass of a duiker, impaled on thorny twigs, safely out of reach of scavengers. But the meat was gone. All that remained in the larder were the skull and a few ragged strips of stinking hide, and these the rain was busy washing clean.

Although hungry, she had had no intention of attacking the hyenas. One, in desperation, she might have tackled, though she preferred smaller game; two were too much for her. She moved off, sliding easily through the dank undergrowth, heading east.

As she went, always listening, always wary, she noted through the rush and roar of wind and water each tiny rustle, each quiver of a leaf. Once a nightjar flew up from under her paws, and a tree hyrax screamed harshly at her from the safety of its hole. A rat shot squeaking across her path—and squeaked no more as her paw flashed out, crushing the tiny skull. It made one mouthful, a tidbit, nothing more.

On she went, out of the woods, across a plantation of young gums, through a garden, close by a farmhouse where an outside light glowed, mosquito-haunted, dazzling in the rain-shot darkness. A dog caught her scent and barked with fear and bravado, but he was locked indoors, and out of her reach.

At last she reached her destination, the farthest eastern point on her beat, a poultry farm where on one glorious occasion she had found a door half latched. She licked her lips, remembering.

But the farmer had learned a hard lesson. That night all was fenced, locked, barred. The hens and turkeys cackled and gobbled with fright as she circled slowly round the pens. Once she wheeled, on guard, at a strange rattling sound nearby. A porcupine came round a corner, its trailing quills brushing a fence. The leopardess stood, one paw raised, glaring through the veiling rain at the porcupine which stared back, erecting its quills with an almost insolent lack of haste. With quills erect it looked enormous. It was full grown, and the quills reached

a height of three feet. This time it was the leopardess who gave way. She prowled off angrily, tail
twitching; her thwarted appetite was growing, her
temper worsening. Above her head an eagle owl
hooted, as if in mockery.

The poultry farm was a failure. She moved away,
faster now, toward the Langata Forest. She had one
main road to cross, but there was no traffic to avoid.
The deserted road streamed with water and already
waterfalls cascaded down the banks on either side,
eating away at the earth. Frogs croaked happily in
the ditches.

Once inside the forest the rain was less noticeable.
Almost at once she scented baboon and she weaved
her silent deadly way from tree to tree closer and
closer to the enticing smell. Baboons, she knew, do
not wander at night. They take to the trees and stay
together, the tough old males, the watchdogs, taking
the low branches, while the younger baboons and
females huddle overhead. The leopard is their arch
enemy.

And so it was that night. But the leopardess had
not yet reached the tree when she heard the scream
of a panic-stricken baboon, followed immediately
by a throaty growl, and a chorus of barks and
screeches.

She crept forward, nose wrinkled wickedly, ears
flattened, and found herself suddenly face to face
with a male leopard twice her size. Blood dripped
from the crushed head of the baboon held in his
mouth. He dropped the baboon and snarled vicious-

ly, baring bloodstained canines in a furious grimace and crouching ready to spring.

The leopardess backed off. Leopards hunt alone and jealously guard their districts. Here, in the forest, two districts overlapped, but the leopards seldom met. Once, briefly, she had welcomed the male, who had become her mate. Now they met as enemies, and she was no match for him.

Hunger gnawed within her, outweighing her anger. But her luck was due to change. She crossed a narrow path, made by small hoofs, and the scent was fresh.

Keeping low, she glided along near the path from bush to bush, cutting corners, green-gold eyes scanning the darkness. Then, nearing her prey, she burst from cover at incredible speed. The bush buck, tripping through a drift of sodden leaves, had no time to swerve aside. Her teeth crunched down through hide, flesh and bone.

Here was food for a feast. The leopardess feasted. Then, making use of her powerful muscles, she dragged the remains high into a tree where the torn sightless body hung limply across a bough. To this she would return. Now, with dawn not far off, it was time to make for home.

Slowly, for she had eaten well, and even she could tire, she headed southwest. By the time she reached the Elliotts' land the rain had stopped. The light was growing, and the clouds parted sufficiently to allow a glimpse of rising watery sun. The leopardess padded along until she reached a gap in the hedge, slid through the trees, paused beneath a window for a tantalizing whiff of dog, then headed down the plot. Home was not far away, and she was filled with well-being.

She drank at a pool, leaped a bank, and padded over short springy grass. The fresh smell of the rain-washed earth intoxicated her. As she entered a wood she startled a family of monkeys. They followed her, calling rude names, but she had eaten well and ignored them. A massive tree caught her eye and she poured herself up the trunk and settled herself on a broad low bough. A ray of sun fell warmly on her back. She began to groom her fur.

3

Karen Goes Tracking

Karen was awake with the birds next morning.

She draped her dressing gown round her shoulders
and skipped over to the window, taking as few steps
as possible on the cold wood-inlay floor. The rain
had stopped but the clouds still lay thick and gray
over the Ngong Hills, wet-blanketing the sky. The
rain pipe near her window gurgled cheerfully and
drips ping-ponged down from the gutters onto the
rounding honeysuckle, which was already hung with
a thousand raindrop prisms. From the woods which
bordered Mrs. Liversedge's land came a sudden outburst of sound, a scolding chatter which Karen knew
well. There were often troops of monkeys in the
woods, the white-ruffed Sykes or the small black-
faced Vervet; something, it seemed, had disturbed
them.

The chattering went on in short bursts, as if the monkeys were watching the progress of some intruder through the woods. Then it stopped as suddenly as it had started, and Karen turned her attention to the scene before her. The lawn was covered with brown leaves and strips of rusty bark beaten down from the eucalyptus trees which grew behind the encircling hedge. A bulbul sang from the top of the telephone pole; an amethyst sunbird hovered among the honeysuckle. The air was cold and smelled deliciously of wet earth. Karen sniffed luxuriously.

There was something odd going on among the leaves on the lawn. Some of them were behaving in a strange, unleaflike manner. Here and there a leaf would suddenly shoot forward an inch or so, as if propelled by an impulsive puff of wind. Karen craned forward on the window seat to watch more closely. All at once she knew the reason.

The lawn was covered with thousands of dead leaves; it was also covered with innumerable little brown frogs which had appeared, as was their habit, out of nowhere to greet the rain. One baby frog at the edge of the grass jumped manfully out onto the damp gravel path. It struggled through a puddle and hiccuped on toward the floor bed.

"Where on earth do they come from?" puzzled Karen. She was reminded of those Japanese paper flowers which expand when placed in water. "And where do they all go? In England it rains cats and dogs. Perhaps in Kenya it rains frogs and toads!"

As if in answer to her second question, a robin

chat appeared from under a hibiscus bush and gobbled up the frog. And then Karen noticed something else.

Along the edge of the flower bed under her bedroom window there were a number of deep imprints. The marks were rounded and blunt, and there was no claw impression; they were quite unlike the long, more angular print left by the dogs, although they were just as large, if not larger. They showed up plainly in the moist red-brown earth.

"Crumbs, something pretty big must have been prowling round the house last night!" Karen nodded to her reflection, dimly seen in the windowpane. "And not so long ago, either, or the rain would have washed the prints away. Now, what could it have been?"

The animal names which came immediately to mind were not the sort her mother would have welcomed in her garden. Karen stilled her thoughts and hushed her conscience. It was a morning to be up and doing; any excuse would serve. She felt at least twice as alive as usual and the normal Sunday routine stretched uninvitingly in front of her. It therefore became of great importance that she investigate the mysterious footprints.

So Karen made a face at the freshly ironed Sunday dress hanging from her closet door and climbed happily back into Saturday's jeans. She pulled a sweater over her tousled head and hunted out her gum boots from where they lay, spattered with dried mud from the last rains, neglected in a corner of the closet. She slipped her arms into a waterproof jacket and zipped it up to her neck. Her hair was soon twisted up, unbrushed, into its accustomed ponytail, and she tied a spotted cotton scarf over her head to hide any deficiencies. Then she was ready.

She glanced at her clock. It was barely a quarter to seven. The house would not be stirring for a while. On Sundays breakfast was an hour later than usual, and Joshua did not arrive until seven-thirty. But if she went through the house to let herself out at the back door or front she would disturb the dogs, and this she did not want to do.

Carefully she removed the row of carved wooden animals which decorated her windowsill and placed them on her dressing table.

Then she opened her window as far as it would go and pushed aside the honeysuckle which swung down from the roof in great loops. She climbed from the window seat over the sill and down onto the flower bed, avoiding the cacti which her mother always planted beneath bedroom windows. (In Kenya there is a special kind of burglar known as a polefisher who hooks his booty out through open windows. Cactus, Mrs. Elliott vowed, was an excellent burglar deterrent. Karen made a mental note that a few more cactus plans were needed in that particular spot if anything at all was to be deterred.)

Once outside she knelt down, disregarding mud and puddles, and peered at the fascinating footprints. They looked even larger from such close quarters. And, as she hoped, they continued clearly right across the flower bed and down behind the house under the jacaranda trees where the grass was scanty. Her face flushed from kneeling and excitement, Karen began to follow the trail.

With lordly disregard for the fence around the vegetable garden, the unknown animal had obligingly walked straight across the soft, well-hoed earth, where the rain had battered down the feathery carrot tops and patched the few remaining lettuces with mud. The young pawpaw trees which Karen's mother had grown from seed, and which were just beginning to fruit, were round-shouldered from the buffeting of the wind.

Karen picked a fistful of fat orange fruit from the Cape gooseberry bushes, peeled back their papery wrappers, and chewed happily. She flung up her arms and stretched, flexing every muscle in her strong young body, reveling in the stillness of the early morning scene and the freshness that the rain had brought to the garden. She longed to sing or shout, but she was too near the rondavels which housed Joshua and Mungai.

When she reached the tangle of bush and long grass beyond the vegetable garden she came to a halt. If she plunged in there she was sure to get in a mess, and a mess on Sunday meant trouble.

"To go or not to go, that is the question," chanted Karen. But she already knew the answer. She plunged.

Karen's land was roughly divided into four parts. The first, close to the house, was smoothly grassed. There were gay flower beds, neatly trimmed hedges and shady trees to make a pleasant setting for the old stone cottage. Next came an area where the grass was rough, and left unwatered, but was still kept short. Here Mrs. Elliott planted flowering shrubs and trees but no attempt was made at excessive tidiness; the dogs might dig for mole rats and bury bones unchecked, and the children do as they wished.

Further down the plot, beyond the servants' houses, the vegetable garden and the chicken run, came a third section. It sloped gently away from the house and was thickly covered with bushes, self-seeded trees, long grass and weeds which towered over Karen's head. Here lived the small wild creatures—dik-dik and duiker, porcupine and hedgehog, mongoose and zorilla, mole rats and plump striped mice, while birds nested in the safety of the thickets. The soil was good red coffee soil, and Mr. Elliott planned one day to clear the bush and plant coffee; but Karen was glad that this was still a dream, as it was her favorite part of the plot. She had several blinds among the bushes and under trees, and here she would lie by the hour, as still as any lizard, to watch the birds and wild creatures.

The remaining stretch of land at the bottom of the slope was flat, and the soil was stony and poor. Vlei grass grew in wiry clumps and here Candytuft, Karen's pony, grazed. Richard's land, where Candytuft was stabled, lay to the left, and the thickly treed plot to the right belonged to Mrs. Liversedge. Beyond all three plots lay a golf course, and beyond again, some miles away, could be seen the wild wooded slopes of the great hills, the Ngongs, Masai territory, where buffalo still lived and lion were seen.

It was into the third section, Karen's "jungle," that she now plunged. Where the ground was overgrown it was no longer possible to trace the footprints. Karen cast about to left and right. Her boots were soon running with water, her jacket and jeans were watermarked, and strands of hair escaped from the prison of her scarf to fall damply over her forehead as she pushed her way through the rain-spangled bushes. Then, to her delight, she picked up the trail again under a silver wattle tree where the grass grew sparsely and the earth was moist. Weaver birds' woven nests, built one upon the other, dangled from the upper branches, and Karen stopped to chirp to the birds in their yellow and black livery as they popped in and out of their front doors above her head. As she ducked under the wattle's lower branches she brushed against the powderpuff flowers. Their faint sweet fragrance clung to her as she moved on, and specks of yellow pollen dusted her shoulders.

Now she was following a narrow winding path, one of the trails made by the animals which lived in the bush. Once she paused to let an enormous toad lollop out of the way. Another time her eye was caught by a puff adder's brittle discarded skin.

"Yikes! I must come back for that," Karen promised herself; but at the moment she had something else on her mind. In case the puff adder was still around she went warily, keeping her eyes open for more than a footprint.

A little further on, a jerky movement among the undergrowh brought her to a stop. A tortoise came pushing its way through a forest of sun-starved stalks, plodding on stumpy legs which slipped and skidded on the muddy patches. Its flat back was mud-colored, and its head was yellowish and snake-like.

Karen was delighted. For a moment she allowed herself to be distracted from her quest; she reached for the tortoise. The yellow head snapped back into the shell with an odd sideways motion. A bright reptilian eye stared at Karen coldly and she hesitated, her hand poised above the shell. She could not have imagined being frightened of a tortoise, but this one had the tense look of a creature about to strike. Then, quickly, Karen seized the tortoise round its middle. She pulled off her head scarf with her free hand and placed the tortoise in the center, tying the four corners together to make a sling. Swinging the scarf from one hand, Karen continued down the path, while the tortoise continued to plod on in his spotted cotton prison, eternally taking one step forward and slipping one back.

Emerging finally from the bush onto grass which was short and springy she gazed around, fearing this time that the trail was lost for good. A plopping sound near at hand startled her. Water? Of course, the old murram pit. Karen started forward, slipping and stumbling like the tortoise on the wet turf, and a heron flew up, long legs trailing limply.

The murram pit, from which the gravel for the drive and other paths had been dug years before, soon yawned in front of her. Except in the very driest weather a small scummy pool lingered at the bottom of the pit. The night's heavy downpour had cleaned out the scum and left a fair-sized pond. A frog plunged into the water at Karen's approach, causing the musical "plop" which had attracted her attention. Spiky green leaves were already beginning to thrust themselves up at one corner of the pool. Was there ever magic quite so potent as the rain of Africa? thought Karen. It waves a wand, and the world is green.

"All the fuss they make in books about turning princes into frogs and ogres into mice! In Africa twice a year a desert turns into a jungle!"

A stretch of bare brown soil, more murram than earth, led down to the water. Here she once more picked up the trail.

"Boy, oh boy, I'm getting good at this," said Karen. "Just a natural-born bushwoman, that's me."

The animal had paused to drink at the pool. A particularly clear footprint showed right at the water's edge. Then the creature had turned to the right, to the foot of the little cliff where the shovels, pickaxes and jembes had worked so busily. The cliff was six feet high and very muddy. Karen turned aside and scrambled round behind the pit, her face glowing from her efforts.

Right at the edge of the cliff one last pugmark showed, where the animal had landed after its leap. Now what could leap like that, Karen pondered?

All at once her throat felt dry, and small cold fingers played a scale up and down her spine. Clearly inside her head she heard her mother's voice saying: "Karen—are you being sensible?" Then she shrugged. "It's just a game I'm playing," she told a fiscal shrike which was noisily resenting her intrusion. "You don't have to scold me. It's a lovely morning. I'm having *fun*. That's all."

What could happen here, on her own land, in broad daylight? And she had seen Ajax scale the cliff. He boosted himself up with a kick and a scrabble. It wasn't as if she were really going to come across the creature she was tracking.

Now the grass grew thickly once more. The footprint pointed toward the woods on Mrs. Liversedge's boundary. Karen trotted in small circles, swinging her tortoise, hoping to find another print somewhere where the ground was bare of cover. But the turf gave away no secrets.

By the time she reached the fence she was panting, and she was glad to perch like a thrush on one of the cedarwood posts and catch her breath. She gazed longingly in the direction of the wood but she was more than a little shy of Mrs. Liversedge, whose eyes were as fierce as a falcon's. Was trespassing really trespassing at that time of day? She could see birds flitting among the trees, and the morning was merry with their songs.

The sun blinked down at her with a watery eye through a hole in the clouds, but away across the fields a gray mist of rain was falling. A wedge of rainbow glimmered enticingly at the edge of the mist. Karen looked back toward the house. She could see thin columns of smoke going up, like messages from her mother, from the wood-burning stove which heated water for her own household, and from the brick fireplace shared by Joshua and Mungai. People were astir; soon the dogs would be released, and soon her mother would discover her absence. It was time she returned, but without a second glance she slipped through the barbed-wire strands of the fence and sped toward the wood.

As she reached the trees a harsh chattering, startlingly loud in the quiet of the morning, halted her. The monkeys again! Karen had forgotten them. She went forward more slowly and as soundlessly as she could. Where were the monkeys? Had she disturbed them—or was her quarry still about? She slipped cautiously round a huge gum tree, its trunk showing smooth and bare through the rags of red bark. And stopped dead in her tracks.

Facing her in the fork of a tree only ten yards away crouched a leopard.

4

Consequences

A ray of sunlight gilded the leopard's coat, polished the black rosettes, and haloed its great cat's head. It had been grooming its fur; one paw was still raised and was slowly lowered. The greenish-amber eyes, with their pinpoint pupils, narrowed and blinked. The muscles tensed in the powerful shoulders.

Karen stood motionless, watching the leopard. And the leopard crouched motionless, watching in its turn.

Then it sneezed. Karen couldn't have been more surprised if it had spoken to her. It shook its head, as if bothered by a fly, and twitched its long cat's whiskers. Then down went the head and the leopard licked its deadly paw with a rose-pink tongue. Water dripped from the leaves around, birds sang and, clearly and warmly, Karen heard the sound of the leopard purring. It was a well-fed, contented leopard; it had taken her measure and dismissed her as unimportant.

Life flooded back into Karen's limbs. Pins and needles pricked her fingers and toes. It was as if her blood had paused in its constant circulating, leaving her chilled and stiff; and then recommenced its work, filling her once more with tingling warmth. As smoothly and slowly as she could, she took a step backwards. And then another, feeling behind her each time with a cautious toe. The leopard continued its toilet.

She had nearly rounded the giant gum and the leopard was only partly in sight, when three things happened. The monkeys, hidden in the trees, chattered furiously once more; a dog barked loudly nearby; and the rain, which had been blowing steadily nearer, swept over the wood, dousing the sun's faint rays and blotting out Karen's view of the leopard. She had a hazy impression of a heavy spotted form disappearing in the opposite direction before she turned and ran for the fence, whistling shrilly as she went.

For the dog's bark had been only too familiar. Ajax was out for his morning's adventure, and the last thing Karen wanted was that Ajax should get involved with the leopard.

By the time Karen reached the path through the bush her jacket was dark with damp. Rain dripped from her forehead to her nose, from her nose to her chin, and from her chin it seeped soggily down her neck. A lock of hair flopped wet and miserable in front of her eyes and blurred her vision.

As luck would have it, she met Ajax in the narrowest section of the path. Ajax was full of joy and love at finding her. He was also as wet as if he had been swimming, and his shaggy legs and plumy tail were nicely muddied.

Karen dodged and yelled at him, and succeeded only in losing her balance. She sat down heavily, dropping the tortoise, half on the path and half in a thorny bush, while Ajax lavished kisses on her cheeks and tiny fluffy seeds parachuted down on her head and shoulders and clung to her jeans.

Karen struggled to her feet, groping for the tortoise as she did so. There would be no avoiding trouble now. She was wet, muddy and desperately untidy. And today was Sunday, and church was at eleven o'clock.

Clutching her scarf she ran on again toward the house, Ajax frolicking at her heels. Her wet jeans rubbed the calves of her legs and she could feel the prickle of burrs in her socks and the trickle of rain behind her ears. In the scarf the tortoise fought the air with its tough little feet, scrabbling at nothing. I'll show it to Richard, thought Karen. He'll know if tortoises are ever poisonous.

But even while she laid plans for the tortoise and tried to marshal her excuses to forestall the inevitable row, her thoughts strayed. Warm in her mind was her memory of the great golden cat purring in the pale sunshine. She had at that moment no sense of fear, of danger escaped; that would come later. And then she thought: If they scold me for being in a mess, they may forget to ask me why I was out! The footprints would wash away in the rain, and the leopard in the tree would be her own special property.

"I'll tell Richard," said Karen. "But not Mummy. She would only worry. It would be kinder *not* to tell her."

It was Ajax, of course, who precipitated the row.

"Whoops!" gasped Karen, clutching at him with her spare hand as he burst at her heels into Joshua's clean bright kitchen. "Joshua, grab him!"

But it was too late. Karen's boots were muddy, but Ajax's paws were muddier still, and when he was excited he seemed to have at least eight legs, and paws to match. All these paws skidded in different directions over the polished kitchen floor. Moreover, he was happy as well as excited—the coming of the rains affected Karen and Ajax in much the same way—and when he was happy he wagged. The very first sweep of his wet and feathery tail sent the milk jug flying from the counter. It was at this moment that Mrs. Elliott entered the room.

"Karen!" said Karen's poor mother.

To make matters worse, Ajax got as far as the dining room before he was captured and ejected, and found time for one really good, soul-satisfying shake, spattering the neatly laid breakfast table and the cream-painted walls, and even sending a rash of muddy splashes across the white ceiling. The table and walls were quickly put to rights, but the spots on the ceiling remained for a long time to remind Karen of the "Day of the Leopard," as she mentally termed it. Her mother said it reminded her of prickly heat, and made her feel itchy to look at it.

Joshua alone was amused by the commotion and this was noble of Joshua, thought Karen, since she caused him so much extra work. Karen herself was bustled away to be bathed and rubbed and arrayed in clean Sundayish garments, and breakfast was a stiff, silent meal.

Then, halfway through breakfast, the sinister tortoise (which Karen had dumped in one corner of the kitchen, still entangled in her head scarf) managed to extricate itself. It had crawled as far as Joshua's bare feet before he spied it, and his yells of terror so startled the Elliotts that Karen's mother spilled her coffee and her father rose so quickly that he tripped over his own feet and banged his elbow painfully on the sideboard. This time Jenny was the one who laughed.

It took some time to calm Joshua down; tortoises, it seemed, were considered by his tribe to bring the worst kind of bad luck. Karen was sorrier about this than anything else, since Joshua was so often her friend and ally. Coffee and food were cold by the time the family returned to the breakfast table, the tortoise having been popped in a box and banished to the veranda.

It was therefore a much-chastened Karen who sat in church beside her mother some hours later. She wore a prim blue dress and her coat was gray. Perched on her head was her Sunday hat, white straw with blue cornflowers, and her well-disciplined ponytail, tied with a blue ribbon, poked aggressively out from under it. "I must look just like a cart horse at a fair!" thought Karen, sticking out her lower lip. "All groomed and curry-combed." But it was no good feeling rebellious. She had caused enough rumpus. The rest of the day she must lie low.

All during the service Karen's thoughts strayed to the leopard. Being night prowlers and wary beasts, they are rarely seen even when they are plentiful. This was a first time for Karen. She hugged the experience to herself, although she was ready now to admit that she had been rash in following the fresh footprints. She had seen enough tracks to have had a pretty good idea of what she was following. She had been lucky; it would be unsafe to take it for granted that a leopard would flee from a chance intruder. "A startled leopard leaps in one of two directions," she had read. "Either away from you, or at you."

Yet her heart rejoiced. And she sang the last hymn at the top of her voice, just to relieve her feelings. "All things bright and beautiful," caroled Karen. "All creatures great and small." It was one of the Vicar's favorite hymns; he too was a naturalist.

The service over, people streamed out of church, huddling into raincoats and struggling to put up umbrellas in too small a space. The usual exchange of greetings and gossip was cut short as everyone dashed to the cars. On the porch Karen bumped into Richard, almost unrecognizable in gray flannel suit, white shirt and dark tie.

"Richard!" She clutched at his arm and beamed at him. "I was looking for you. Do come back with us. I've got something special to tell you. Your father's talking to the Vicar. They've started on warblers and cisticolas and they'll be simply ages."

"OK, mosquito," said Richard. "I've nothing much to do." He caught his father's eye and semaphored his departure, then ran after Karen to clamber into the back seat of the Elliotts' car.

"Phew, what a day!" Mr. Elliott removed his dripping hat and frowned at it. There seemed nowhere suitable to put it. On the floor he would tread on it, and on the seat it would puddle. Mrs. Elliott took it out of his hand and held it on her plastic-coated lap.

"We look forward to the rains for months," continued Mr. Elliott. "Then the moment they start we wish they were over."

"Oh no we don't. Speak for yourself." And Mrs. Elliott glanced contentedly out of the window with her gardener's eye at the freshening grass and the rich red-brown earth greedily soaking up the rain.

Karen and Richard were talking about the Easter holidays, which were only one week away. Three weeks of freedom from school!

"Remember I showed you that letter yesterday?" Richard said now. "About the Duncans? Well, it's OK. They'll be coming Thursday night. Angus is in my form. He's a brainy type, but great value. But I don't think he's got much time for girls. Small ones, anyway! Jock, now, he's only a youngster, about your age, Karen. He's a bit of a clown."

"Does that mean you'll be busy all the time? I mean, what about me? Can I come over same as usual?"

Richard looked at her. "Don't be girlish, Karen. It doesn't suit you. Of course you'll come over, you always do. Jock'll probably be glad to see you. I told you. He's your age."

Karen frowned down at her Sunday-gloved hands. "Boys the same age as girls are so much younger!" she burst out. "And we have things to do. You know, for our collections—and the sort of things we always do."

"Well, we'll do 'em, Karen. Don't get het up over nothing," said Richard. He's pacifying me, thought Karen. Patting me on the head and throwing me a bone. Boys! She chewed a glove finger.

"It's high time you both did some work on your collections," said Mrs. Elliott peaceably, twisting around in the front seat. Karen and Richard collected rocks, shells, wild flowers, feathers, snakeskins, and anything else they could find, or acquire. They also kept a sort of diary, recording any information they found out for themselves about animals and birds. There was always a heap of valuable material waiting to be docketed and put away, covered in dust, and threatened by Mrs. Elliott, who enjoyed the collecting but thought a little more work should be done on the results.

The rain swooshed down on the car and splashed out from under the wheels like a bow wave. Mr. Elliott drove carefully along the slippery road. The ditches edging the road, so dry and dusty the day before, were already brimming with frothing racing water, while rivulets poured down the eroded banks and splashed into the ditches, adding to the flood. The windshield wipers worked with frantic haste, gasping at their work, as if they knew they had been set an impossible task.

To everyone's relief the rain had slackened by

the time they reached the house. They were able to dash for the veranda without too much damage to Sunday hats and well-pressed trousers.

The dogs were waiting on the veranda. Tina rose to greet them from where she sat, curled as small as possible, on the doormat. Ajax was sitting on his elbows in what Karen called "a typical place." Most of him was high and dry, but his tail lay limply in the only puddle to be found on the veranda floor.

"Don't let Ajax in," said Mrs. Elliott hastily. Tina, in her motherly anxiety to return to her pups, slid through a smaller door opening than Karen would have believed possible. The rest of the party followed, leaving Ajax, all hurt eyes and long nose, breathing gustily against the French windows.

"Well, what was it you wanted to tell me?" asked Richard, once inside the living room. And, to show there was no ill feeling, he grinned at her, his rare delightful grin that normally won Karen over. Mr. Elliott was changing his shoes and Mrs. Elliott had disappeared in search of Jenny, left in the care of Mungai's daughter, Wanjiku. The house smelled enticingly of roasting chicken with herb-and-sausage stuffing.

But Karen was still feeling ruffled. He's so grown-up but he doesn't know everything, she thought. Not about my leopard. She flung her hat on the sofa and rubbed her chin where the elastic chafed her. "Oh," she said. "That. I didn't mean tell. I meant show. Half a sec." And she went to fetch the strange tortoise.

And if she didn't tell Richard, there really seemed no reason to tell anyone. Although leopards were not uncommon in the neighborhood this was the first, as far as Karen knew, that had visited her own garden and she had no reason to suppose it would come again. She began to weave stories around the leopard, to use it as a source of daydreams. It replaced the lion cub that had previously been her dream companion.

"What if it were tame?" dreamed Karen. "What if I had brought it up by hand, and then it returned to its wild life. But it came back to see me."

School having closed for the holidays, Angus and Jock Duncan duly arrived the following Thursday, after a week of teeming rain. Karen went over to meet them on the morning of Good Friday, hoping for the best. Angus was tall and dark. He had a long mournful face and strong marked eyebrows which he practiced raising one at a time over the rim of his spectacles. He did this now as Karen was introduced, making her feel like a specimen kept for its oddity value.

"What have we here?" said Angus to Richard.

"A human child," grinned Richard.

"Indubitably," said Angus.

But after that the older boys concentrated on their own affairs, and soon Richard hurried Angus off to the stables, leaving Karen, to her indignation, alone with Jock.

Jock was not a bit like his brother. He was freckled and roly-poly, his hair had a reddish tinge, and he was as friendly as a puppy. He too wore spectacles. They sat a little crooked on his nose, and he explained this almost at once to Karen.

"I have odd ears, see?" he said. "One is joined on higher than the other."

"How nice," said Karen, politely.

"Yes, isn't it?" said Jock. "I can waggle them, too." And this he did, until Karen just had to giggle, because she didn't know what to say.

After that, it seemed the only thing to do was to take Jock back home to meet her mother and sister and, more important, view the puppies. She introduced each one, and explained their names.

"You see, Alsatian pups always look like bear cubs, so this one, the biggest, is Bruin. The smallest is Wee Bear. This one, the whiny one, is Grizzly Bear. And this one, who goes off by himself and hides in corners and is always turning up missing, is Nandi Bear—you know, after that creature they say haunts the Nandi Hills. The girl is Honey Bear and this sweetie"—here she picked up a white puppy and tickled its chin—"is Poley Bear."

"I didn't know you could have white Alsatians," said Jock. "Are you sure he's real?"

"He's a throwback. So clever of Tina. Isn't he gorgeous?" said Karen. "The Kennel Club frowns at white Alsatians—but I bet they wouldn't frown at Poley! Who could? They all have very grand names, as well as their bear names, which they can use on Sundays."

Jock was very taken with Poley Bear and returned him reluctantly to the basket in the store-room where the puppies now lived. They could only be taken out of doors in between rainstorms, and Mrs. Elliott was already praying for the day when they would be old enough to go to new homes— in a week or so.

Jock went home to lunch at twelve o'clock, dodging through drenching rain without a coat but with an old gray felt hat pulled well down over his head. The hat had a zebra skin band and Karen soon learned that it was one of Jock's most treasured possessions. Where Jock went, there went Jock's hat.

Left alone, Karen wandered into the dining room and watched her mother spoon stewed apples and custard into Jenny's mouh, which gaped like a baby sparrow's.

"Don't forget we're going out to tea this afternoon," said Mrs. Elliott, after some minutes' silence.

"No," said Karen.

"Jock seems a very nice boy," continued her mother. She glanced sideways at Karen and went on unconsciously opening and closing her own mouth in sympathy with Jenny.

"Yes," said Karen.

"And it's nice for Richard to have Angus— someone his own age."

"Oh—poof," said Karen.

She got up and retired to her own bedroom, where she brushed her hair hard without being reminded, just to spite it. Then, as her own lunch was still not ready, she flung herself down on her bed and gave herself up to her newest, and best, daydream. There she was, the only woman game warden in Kenya;

and there was Richard, her assistant game warden, looking at her admiringly. And there was her tame leopard, her famous tame leopard, who accompanied her everywhere. Her beautiful, gentle, golden *friendly,* leopard.

5

Baboons

It was the baboon's dying scream that triggered the attack.

The male leopard, padding his silent way home at dawn on Saturday, came upon the baboon sitting alone in a clearing near the edge of the forest. Raindrops clung to the leaves and plunked down on the sodden earth. Each blade of grass was glazed with water, and silvered by the scant rays of early morning sun which filtered through the eucalyptus trees. Other baboons stirred in the trees. The early riser, for once unwary, yawned, scratched at her shaggy chest, then poked hopefully beneath a rotting log for grubs.

The leopard had eaten but still inside him there remained an unfilled space, baboon size. He crept closer. Closer.

When he was within a few yards of the unsuspecting beast, he erupted from the undergrowth, bounding forward to seize the baboon by the neck. The baboon jerked forward, head twisted sideways, legs flailing the air as she made a compulsive effort to escape. Her teeth snapped at nothing. Her lips writhed back and her gums showed pink as she screamed in pain and terror for the last time in her short life.

Briefly there was silence. Dead silence. The broken body twitched on the ground and the leopard stood guard over it, panting and watchful. The clearing seemed empty but for the killer and the killed.

Then all bedlam broke lose in the clearing.

Down from the trees, furious, grimacing, swung the old male baboons.

They were the sentries, the guardians of the troop. Caught napping, taken for once off guard, they flared in almost human anger and, instead of fleeing from their enemy, they swarmed at him from all sides, barking, screeching, their huge canine teeth bared in rage. Behind them came the females and youngsters, swept up in the mad fury which had infected their leaders.

The leopard drew back on his haunches, thick neck arched, long tail lashing behind him. He glared at the mob with hate-filled eyes, spat, and reared up, threatening them with teeth and steel-tipped paws; but his snarl came thin through the crescendo of their barking, as they egged themselves on with ever-increasing noise.

They surrounded him and leaped from sides and rear, tearing at his flanks and back, dodging his savage teeth and flashing claws. He lashed out with both front paws, weaving his head from side to side. SLASH—a baboon screamed as half an ear was torn from his head. SLASH—a baboon ducked, sprang and fastened his teeth in golden fur. SLASH —a gray-furred form thudded against a tree trunk and lay still. Snarls ripped from his open bloody mouth with every rasping breath.

They landed on his back, hacking at his neck with huge teeth, and he rolled over, crushing those that did not leap away, and scooped with all four paws at the nearest baboon, striving to disembowel him. His claws went home, and blood spurted, spattering all about, adding edge to anger. Tufts of fur, gray and golden, littered the reddening earth.

They surged back at him, driving him away from the body of his victim and, realizing this, he sprang forward, scattering bodies right and left, in an attempt to regain his prize. But the action enraged the baboons still further. They swarmed over the leopard like monstrous mosquitoes, jabbing, rending the gold and ebony skin on which blood showed, scarlet, baboon blood and his own.

Crippled baboons withdrew from the battle. One lay dead, skull crushed, beside the lichen-covered log. But still they fought, and the sound of the battle rang through the forest, while the birds withheld their song and small creatures cowered in the undergrowth, still as the death they feared.

And the leopard was in retreat.

He made for the trees, half-blinded by blood welling from a tear across the corner of his eye. The baboons raced with him, one, for a brief chaotic moment, riding him like a jockey before tumbling to earth, one swinging from his tail, while the others snatched and scratched and the females screamed with hysterical hate. They swarmed with him up the trunk, harrying him from branch to branch, mauling whatever part of him came within their reach. He turned and struck, and a baboon catapulted from the tree and crunched down into the clearing.

He stayed then, at bay, crouching with his back against the tree trunk, spitting at his enemies; and they, nearing exhaustion, paused in their attack. Leopard and baboons panted open-mouthed, blood and saliva sliming their teeth and matting their fur. The forest waited.

Then the leopard leaped, seized a young baboon from his ringside perch, and leaped once more, away from his tormentors. Over their heads, into the next tree, he sailed, and twigs and leaves and raindrops showered down as he landed heavily, slipped, regained his balance, and sprang again, away from the battlefield, from bough to bough and tree to tree, until he reached the edge of the forest and launched himself out of his tree and onto the ground. He raced away, bleeding from a hundred tears and scratches, his prey gripped in his teeth, and the baboons hurled sticks and stones after him. Then they huddled together and licked their wounds, and barked and chattered with excitement, and knew briefly the glory of triumph.

Slowly the fight-haze died from their eyes. Their chattering quietened. Mothers began to groom their babies, hungry youngsters began the eternal search for food. The old dog baboons moved painfully to their posts around the troop. They investigated their wounds with inquisitive fingers and cradled damaged limbs against their hairy bodies. Some crawled away to die.

But the leopard kept going.

By the time the human world was on the move he was well away from the forest and his old territory. He paused, briefly, in a plantation of young gums, to eat his kill. Then on again he went, slinking from cover to cover, avoiding roads and houses, working deeper and deeper into the country of the young leopardess. Soon he had reached a thickly wooded plot, overgrown and neglected, where trees, bushes, new growth and old sisal, struggled together to reach the sun. He found a tree large enough and broad enough to serve his purpose and went up it with one liquid leap. Here he licked his wounds and rested, besieged by flies which came in swarms to torment him.

For days he would be stiff and clumsy. And this meant he would go short of food. (He was lucky to be alive, but this he did not know. The baboon troop he tangled with was small. Many a leopard has been torn to pieces by the baboons on which he sought to prey.) But all the leopard knew was pain, and anger. He had eaten but hunger would return. He would need to find his food the easy way.

It was at this moment that he heard, not far away, the excited yapping of a small dog.

Dogo Liversedge, out for his morning stroll, had come across something which interested him.

6

Hide and Seek

On Saturday morning the Elliotts were still at breakfast when a visitor arrived. The dogs barked, feet stumped up the veranda steps, a loud voice called, *"Hodi!"* and Mrs. Liversedge loomed up in the doorway.

Mrs. Liversedge was elderly ("almost a hundred," thought Karen wickedly), but she was still a person to be reckoned with. Tall, heavily built, always tanned a leathery brown, she rode and gardened and patrolled her grounds in high-buttoned snake-proof boots, divided skirt and bush jacket, with a ramshackle felt hat pulled well down over her knot of untidy white hair. She carried a riding crop and usually the scene was completed by Dogo, who strolled at her side the picture of sausage-dog elegance. Today, he was missing.

That, it seemed, was what she had come about.

"Can't find me dog," she said, accepting a cup of coffee and straddling a chair as if it were a horse. "Doesn't like rain—wouldn't wander far in the wet. Went out this morning early. Hasn't come back for his brekker."

"Oh dear," sympathized Mrs. Elliott. She mopped Jenny's eggy chin with one hand and handed her a rusk with the other. "It is so worrying when animals disappear like that. If you need help, I'm sure Karen would be willing to help you look for him. Wouldn't you, dear?"

"Mmm, yes, Mummy, of course I will," said Karen. She was trying not to giggle, which was the way Mrs. Liversedge affected her. As a distraction she gulped down her pineapple juice. A keen glance from her father helped to sober her, and his next words hit her like a shower of cold water.

"Do you think he's been attacked by something, Mrs. Liversedge? A hyena—or a leopard, perhaps? There's a poultry farm not far from here where they've been raided by a leopard recently."

"Dogo went out after seven this morning. Not likely anything would still be about. Still, one can't be sure. You haven't seen him over here?"

Dogo was a familiar figure in dry weather, sitting on the lawn admiring Tina, or playing tug-of-war with Ajax and a stick, a game which usually ended when Ajax tossed his head and swung both stick and dachshund off the ground. But he had not been seen since the rains began.

"Hope he's not caught in a snare." Mrs. Liversedge glared out of the window, upper lip stiff. "Game little chap. Dashed fond of him. Wouldn't want to lose him." She rose creakily to her feet, said an abrupt good-by, and departed as suddenly as she had arrived.

Mr. and Mrs. Elliott exchanged glances. The previous year Ajax had been caught in a wire snare, set by an African to catch one of the small buck which visited the gardens at night. Ajax had been rescued just in time, half strangled. He was big and strong; a small animal like Dogo would not last long if caught by the neck in a noose.

"I'll get Richard to help," said Karen, glad of the excuse. "And Jock. Oh, and Angus too, if he likes." She stuffed her last piece of toast and marmalade into her mouth, and her words were muffled. "We'll all go and play hunt the Dogo through the woods." She picked up her little sister's spoon, one of her shoes and half her rusk from the floor, laid them on the table, and made for the door, happy to start moving, be active, and not think too closely about disappearing dogs and prowling leopards.

Karen discovered Richard and his guests devouring enormous helpings of bacon, eggs and mushrooms, cooked by Kukombe, an elderly African who had worked for Mr. Faulkner for twenty years. Kukombe had kept an eye on Richard since his mother had died. The boys readily agreed to help hunt for the missing dog and, when all the plates had been emptied, Karen led the way back to her own garden.

"We found the mushrooms yesterday afternoon,"

confided Jock, picking his teeth with his little finger. "Scrumptious masses of 'em, in the dairy farm's fields."

"Oh?" said Karen, coldly.

"We called for you, Karen, but you were out with your mother," said Richard.

"So I was," said Karen. "Did you pick any toadstools by mistake?"

"Nope."

"Pity," said Karen.

But it was a beautiful morning, and Karen didn't really feel crotchety. It had rained the night through, and the ground was soaking. A heavy mist still lay in the hollows but overhead the clouds were parting, and cracks of blue could be seen. Rain lilies, like pink and white crocuses, had sprung up overnight among the fresh green grass. It was fun to be out and about in the cool, sweet-smelling air and, although they searched diligently, their spirits were high, and little things set them laughing—dignified Angus, slithering in the mud, arms flailing like a windmill; Richard, giving orders, and stepping unnoticing into a rain-filled hole; and Karen, pushing after Jock through the bushes, receiving a cupful of water full in the face as Jock released a leafy branch too soon.

"You . . . clumsy coot," sputtered Karen.

"Sorry, I'm sure," said Jock. And he swept his old felt hat off his head and made her a deep bow. But five minutes later he tripped over his own feet and knocked her flying.

"Jock!" said Karen dangerously, scrambling out of a bush.

"I have three left feet," said Jock, and wiggled his ears so repentantly that Karen had to laugh. You just couldn't stay angry with Jock.

They started at the boundary hedge and quartered the ground, searching through the trees and scrub until they reached Mrs. Liversedge's lawn. But no smooth brown form appeared, alive or dead—and Richard, for one, was looking for signs of a fight. They hunted back over Karen's land and found Mrs. Liversedge, with Ajax in attendance, searching along the ditch near the road, calling to the missing dog in a voice warm with anxiety, quite unlike her usual mannish tones. She rewarded them with strong peppermints and packed them off again, waving her crop at them and shouting encouragement.

"Poor old Dogo," said Karen. "Where, oh where, can that little dog be?"

Suddenly she stared across the road, where the house was empty and the garden ran wild. The rest of the plot had once been planted with sisal. Sisal plants still showed their saw-edged silvery leaves among the tangle of black wattle, young gums and weeds and creepers of every sort.

"That's where Daddy found Ajax," she reminded Richard. "When he was snared, remember? It's such a jungle, anything could be hidden in there. Do you think we should look?"

"You bet," said Richard. "Hey, look at Ajax!"

Ajax had already crossed the road and was standing on the grassy verge, sniffing curiously at the edge of the trees.

"Think he remembers?" asked Richard.

"Probably after a rat," said Karen.

The boys, who were wearing waterproof jackets, pushed into the sharp-thorned bush ahead of Karen, who wore only a sweater. Even here there were a few narrow paths, animal highways, and they forced their way along one, Ajax taking the lead. The overcrowded trees met and jostled above their heads. It was dark and damp, and smelled not unpleasantly of rotting leaves and fungus. Fallen trees and vines booby-trapped their passage and the heavy atmosphere dampened their spirits and hushed their voices. All of a sudden, Ajax stopped dead.

Angus, next in line, stumbled and almost fell.

"Now, now, dog, watch it," said Angus. "Richard my boy, you know this friend of man better than I do. What's his little trouble?"

Ajax's head came up. The thick fur on his neck bristled. His lips pulled back from his teeth.

Softly, throatily, he began to growl.

From where he lay, draped over the broad horizontal branch of a fig tree, the male leopard glared through the camouflaging leaves at the intruders. He had heard them coming and had flattened himself against the bough, arranging his sinuous body and lying so still he seemed carved from the same wood. His mottled fur merged with the lichenblotched bark. He was still sore and aching from his battle with the baboons; one eye was swollen shut and his ears were in tatters. Flies buzzed over his raw wounds. His temper was savage.

Now he smelled dog, the edible; and man, the enemy. The end of his thick plushy tail stirred among the leaves, and saliva ran in his mouth. The muscles in his shoulders coiled tighter, tensed to spring. His good eye gleamed green in the underwater light admitted by the matted leaves. He bared stained teeth in a silent snarl. He waited.

A few yards more, and the leader would pass below his tree, beneath his branch. A few yards more. . . .

7

Siafu

"Karen!"

Karen, last in line and unable to see what was causing the holdup, started and turned as she heard her name called.

"KAREN! CHILDREN!" The voice came again, a loud commanding voice, from outside the jungle. It had an urgent sound.

"Richard? Hey, someone's calling us. I think we have to go. What's the matter up there anyway?"

"Ajax has the wind up. He won't budge. Did you say we were wanted?"

"Well, someone keeps calling me. I'll have to go. If Ajax is in a dither, p'raps he's smelled a snake or something. Keep your eyes open."

"Kaaaaaaren! KAREN!"

"Look, I've simply got to go." Karen turned in

her tracks and began to struggle back toward the road. Behind her the boys stood indecisive, and Ajax pressed hard against Angus's knees.

"This dog is really worried," Angus spoke quietly to Richard. "I think we should all get out of here."

"What's up?" asked Jock, wriggling impatiently behind Richard's masking back.

"Shut up. We're going back," said Richard flatly. He had been straining his eyes to make out what lay ahead of them. He could see nothing but vegetation, yet his scalp crawled. He turned and, placing his hands on Jock's shoulders, guided him firmly after Karen.

Angus, holding Ajax by his chain collar, pushed after Richard. All at once they began to run, as best they could, ducking under branches and leaping over logs.

Behind them there came a dry rasping cough. And again.

The sound spurred them on. The boys burst out of the bush close on Karen's heels and she turned, startled and cross.

"What's the matter? You don't have to shove!"

But the boys ignored her. "Yah! Did you hear that?" squeaked Jock.

"Yikes!"

"Don't panic, men. Just run for your lives!"

"But what's the matter?" asked Karen.

"Didn't you hear it?"

"Hear what?"

"That sort of cough. Richard, there's only one creature makes a noise like that, isn't there?"

Richard looked soberly at Jock and Angus. "Far as I know."

"But what did you hear?" Karen shook Richard's arm. "Tell me, tell me!"

"We heard a cough, Karen. A nasty raspy cough. There was a leopard in there, I'm pretty sure. Ajax was pretty sure, too." And Richard bent down and rubbed hard at Ajax's ears. Ajax lolled his tongue at them.

"A—a—leopard?" Karen caught her breath. She swung round and stared at the wilderness they had just left. "A leopard," she repeated. She took a step forward.

"KAREN. Oh, Karen." Mrs. Liversedge tramped along the opposite side of the road toward them. She waved a stick at them.

"Karen, your mother wants you at home. Joshua has been hunting for you."

"Oh dear. I'd better run," said Karen. She loped away, diving through the gap in the hedge, clearing stumps and small bushes and racing through the long wet grass. Ahead she could hear a commotion. Someone was yelling, Tina was barking furiously, and Karen could hear her mother's voice calling urgently. She ran faster, and her cheeks were scarlet by the time she pushed through the hedge onto the lawn in front of the house. The boys followed her.

An odd sight met their eyes. Mrs. Elliott was sweeping wildly on the veranda with the garden broom, while Joshua flapped at the walls with a duster and every now and then leaped into the air

with a shout. Mungai seemed to be lighting a bon-
fire on the steps. Tina stood on the drive, barking
defiantly, but not approaching.

"Look out, Karen!" Richard spoke sharply as
Karen ran out onto the lawn. *"Siafu!* Millions of
'em."

Karen pulled up short and stared, aghast. All
over the smooth green grass black glistening heaps
of safari ants were erupting from unseen holes, and
near the house the heaps merged into a living carpet
of ants, huge, armor-plated, sharp-pincered ants,
oozing like molten tar toward the house. They were
swarming up the walls, pitch-black against the white
plaster, and spilling over the steps onto the veranda.

Already ants were climbing onto Karen's boots.
She shook her foot.

"Mummy, what happened?" she called. "What do
you want us to do?"

"Oh, sweetie, there you are." Mrs. Elliott paused
in her frantic sweeping. "We mustn't let them get in
the house, we'd never get them out! The back path
is alive with them and your father's gone to town
and I don't know what to do first!"

"I know. Karen, have you got a garden spray?
And some insect killer? Pyrethrum?" It was Richard
who spoke. He gave rapid instructions, sending
Angus and Jock speeding to his own house to fetch
two more sprays, while Karen and Mungai met at
the tool shed and mixed up gallons of insecticide.

Soon Mungai, Richard and Angus were circling
around and around the house, drenching the walls
along the base and near the windows. The ants

curled and writhed and died by the thousands, but still there were thousands more working their way in black belts over the grass and up the walls.

Meanwhile, Jock, armed with another broom, was helping Mrs. Elliott on the veranda, and Joshua went indoors to slam windows and deal with ants that had already found a way in. Her mixing completed, Karen joined Joshua. He had dealt with the living room and dining room and was hard at work in the kitchen. Karen made her way to the bedroom end of the house where she found ants crawling aimlessly along her windowsill. These she sprayed with an aerosol spray kept for mosquitoes. She tiptoed into Jenny's nursery where, incredibly, her small sister lay sleeping, kitten-easy, despite the confusion nearby. Karen made sure no ants had sneaked across to Jenny's cot, or were hidden in the folds of the mosquito net which hung, in the daytime, against the wall.

Then came the storeroom, where the puppies yapped at the tops of their voices. Karen paused to give them each a pat before going on to police her parent's bedroom and, finally, entered the bathroom, which was built behind the kitchen and shared the same stretch of roof.

Quite a number of ants were parading down the white-tiled walls. Karen brushed them into the bath, turned on the taps and swooshed them down the drain. She was just finishing when she realized that from somewhere overhead there was coming a most extraordinary noise, a sort of frantic buzzing roar.

Balancing precariously on the side of the bath,

she opened the small window once again, stuck out her head and looked around. Richard was spraying nearby, and she called to him.

"Richard, hi, Richard, can you hear that awful noise? What on earth is it?"

Richard looked blankly around, wondering who was talking to him, until he spotted Karen's face framed in the window above his head. He frowned as he listened, then looked sharply upwards at the guttering.

"Holy cats, Karen, it's the ants, I mean the bees, I mean the ants are raiding the bees!"

A column of ants about three inches wide had swarmed up the wall unnoticed behind a rain pipe to the opening under the tiles which led to the bees' nest. A few bees zoomed wildly round the hole, buzzing angrily, while on the ground below small furry bee carcasses were already being carried off by the raiders.

Since her work in the house was finished, Karen closed the bathroom window and ran outside where she found her fellow workers, taking a breather. They were standing well back from the house while they gazed upwards and discussed the battle that was going on.

"Wild bees are *kali* enough—you'd think they could defend themselves against a few bloomin' ants!" scoffed Jock. He yelped as a stray ant climbed above his sock and dug its red-hot pincers into his leg.

"Well, can you?" mocked Karen, glad of her gum

boots. She hastily tucked the legs of her jeans down inside her socks for added protection.

"I don't think they stand much of a chance," said Angus, sensibly spraying a circle of ant-killer around the feet of the watchers. "On a cool day like this the bees would mostly have been in the nest. At the rate those ants are going in they would have choked the entrance, and the bees wouldn't be able to get out. And what could they do anyway, except fly away? Sting the ants? Fat chance they'd have. These ants are armored like mini-tanks."

"Well, whose side are we on?" demanded Karen. She was hopping up and down with excitement. "The bees may be nuisances, but they do share our house, and the ants are absolute stinkers. Come on, shock troops, spray the rain pipe as high as you can!"

Richard raised his spray, then stopped, and laughed. "Karen, when I first knew you, you used to rescue flies from spiders' webs and weep over squashed frogs on your drive. You know what? You're getting tough!"

So thick was the column of ants that it was some time before the spraying had effect. Angus stood on a stepladder and sprayed the tiles and gutter as far as he could reach, while Jock swept down dead and dying ants (and bees) with his long-handled broom. By the time they felt satisfied that only a few living ants remained on that side of the house the dreadful muffled buzzing of the trapped bees had died away. The children stood and wondered. Had all the bees died? Or was peace restored in that dark grim hole that must now resemble a slaughterhouse rather than a nest? Karen shivered. She had never found anything to admire in the regimented lives of ants, and it was not pleasant to think of that ferocious horde pouring in on the drowsy unsuspecting bees.

They worked on until they were reasonably sure that all the walls near windows and doorways were drenched in insecticide, and that no new columns of ants were threatening the house. On the lawn, ants still marched and countermarched and a long column was wending its way down the overflow ditch that conducted the bathwater away from the house toward the vegetable garden. For a day or so, people and dogs visiting the garden would have to tread warily; but the house seemed safe.

By this time it was well past noon and Richard, Angus and Jock made their way home to clean themselves up before lunch. They all felt, too, that they would be happier when they had changed their clothes and made quite sure there were no safari ants lurking in socks or shirts. Ants seemed to have a built-in knowledge of just where to bite to produce the maximum of discomfort in the hardest-to-get-at place.

"Now you must all come back to tea," Mrs. Elliott called after them. "You've save our lives, and you must come and be feted."

8

Dogo

When Mr. Elliott arrived home for lunch that day he found a distracted household. Everyone had been too involved in the battle with the ants to think about food. The steak still lay stiff and stark in the refrigerator and the peas were zipped tightly in their pods.

"Oh well, never mind," said Mrs. Elliott, bustling about with Jenny squirming under one arm. "We'll have soup and sandwiches. Oh, dear, do keep this child amused for a while, Karen. She's into everything."

Karen looked around for Ajax, since one of Jenny's favorite games was "horseback" riding, with Ajax for the horse, and Karen holding her on. Ajax liked this game too; when he had had enough he lay down and rolled over, and this was the part Jenny loved best of all.

Tina lay in her favorite place on the rug in the sitting room. Now that the puppies were older she was spending more time away from them. But Ajax was nowhere to be found.

"Oh botheration," said Karen to herself. "I forgot to round him up." Outside the rain leaked down. Karen glanced at her father, deep in a coffee-planter's magazine. She listened to her mother's voice, as she chatted to Joshua in the kitchen, using five words of English to one of Swahili but convinced she was speaking his language. No one seemed to have remembered Ajax. It would be as well to leave things alone and wait for the truant's return, wet and muddy as he was sure to be. Karen resignedly got down on her hands and knees and did her best to take Ajax's place.

"By the way," said Mr. Elliott during lunch, pointing to a small package lying on the sideboard. "You'll never guess what I finally bought this morning."

Mrs. Elliott looked at him, her face still flushed from bustling. "Don't tease, John. I'm far too flustered to play guessing games."

"Open that, will you, Karen?"

Karen unwrapped the package and held up the contents in silence. It was a smoke bomb, designed for use on wild bees.

Mrs. Elliott took it gingerly from Karen, handling it as if she thought it might erupt then and there.

"Congratulations, John! At last. But I think the ants have done the job for you."

"I think we'll use it, just to make sure, if the rain gives over for a bit this evening. I was so proud of remembering it."

Karen too had remembered something.

"Oh crumbs, I quite forgot. We didn't finish our hunt for Dogo. And I never went back to tell Mrs. Liversedge why. I do hope he turned up in one piece. I'll go over and inquire about him when it stops raining."

And then she remembered something else, and fell silent. The leopard. Had there been a leopard in the bush that morning? What had frightened Ajax and what had the boys heard? Surely a lurking leopard and a missing dog on the same day must be more than a coincidence? If she had told someone about seeing the leopard the previous week, would Mrs. Liversedge have watched more carefully over her precious dachshund?

It was at that moment, as if on cue, that a sudden outburst of barking disturbed the luncheon party. Tina poked an inquiring head around the door, and Mr. Elliott threw down his napkin with an annoyed flourish.

"Is that dog out in the rain again? Can we never eat a meal in peace in this house?"

Karen ran to the French doors and peered out onto the veranda. It was typical of Ajax, she felt, not only to stay out in the rain when all well-behaved dogs would have wanted to be indoors, but also to announce his return so noisily. He had no tact.

"Ajax," she grumbled at him. "Bad dog. Where have you been? Sit on the mat and drip. Then we might let you in."

But Ajax would not sit down. Normally, when she scolded, he drooped his ears and lowered his tail and indicated with mournful eyes his complete and utter repentance for his misdeeds. This time he stayed alert and prick-eared. He bounded forward when she spoke, then leaped away to the top of the steps, eyes bright, tail wagging at full speed.

"Oh Ajax, nobody wants to play with you," said Karen. "Sit *down,* you gormless lump, and behave yourself." She moved away but, as she did so, Ajax burst into a new volley of barks. Reluctantly she turned back, and her father came to stand by her side.

"He sounds very excited." Mr. Elliott had recovered from his spurt of bad temper and was watching Ajax with interest.

"He—he's trying to get me to do something," said Karen. Ajax had now come close to the door and was whining and scratching at the doormat as if digging his way in to them.

"Open the door, Karen. Just a little way. Careful, he's soaking wet."

Karen complied. The moment she turned the door handle Ajax was off again to the steps, his head on one side, his body quivering with excitement.

"Yes, he wants us out there." Intrigued now, Mr.

Elliott turned to his wife. "Never a dull moment," he said cheerfully. "I think Karen and I will just pop out and see what this is all about. Don't drink all the coffee while we're gone! Grab my coat for me, Karen, will you, please?"

A few minutes later they were squelching along the path, rain sprinkling their faces, following an excited dog who dashed off ahead of them the moment the door opened. Round the house they went, through the shade trees and down past the vegetable garden. Here Ajax paused for a moment to make quite sure he was being followed before he pranced off again.

"Looks as if he's heading for the old hen coop."

The old hen house had become too eaten away by termites for further patching by handyman Mungai. A new shed and run had been constructed six months previously and the old one had been left in tribute to the white ants. The roof had collapsed and weeds grew tall in the entrance. Ajax stopped at one side of this ramshackle outbuilding and whined once more, pawing at the ground by a hole in the side of the shed.

"Look out now, Karen." Mr. Elliott pushed past her. "It may be a snake, or some savage creature." He bent down in front of the jagged hole, elbowing Ajax out of the way. Ajax stopped whining and sniffed eagerly, and suddenly they heard a new sound, a faint, pain-filled whimper.

"Something's hurt." Mr. Elliott tugged at the rotten wood round the hole, wary of splinters. A board broke off in his hand and carefully he en-

larged the hole. He worked kneeling on the muddy ground, and rain trickled steadily down his intent face. Karen crouched at his side.

When the second board was removed, light seeped into the musty interior. A small, fox-brown form became visible, huddled in a corner among the old nesting boxes. A head was lifted, a queer lopsided head, and one brown eye blinked at them.

"It's Dogo! But oh, look at his poor sad face," gasped Karen in dismay. Dogo's face was swollen like a melon at one side, so that he looked like a bad case of canine mumps. One eye was closed by the swelling, and one paw was held crookedly against the once-smooth coat, now muddied and matted with burrs.

Very gently Mr. Elliott drew the pitiful form toward him. Carefully he lifted the little dog and cradled him in one arm.

"What is it, Daddy? Has he been bitten by a snake?" Karen hovered anxiously around her father while Ajax, his job done, sat down in a puddle and scratched.

"No . . . no, I don't think so. Ah, look at his paw, Karen. That's what's the matter with the poor little chap."

Karen looked, and winced. Protruding from the inside of Dogo's injured front leg was a long grayish-yellow quill. Dogo, adventuring through the bush when out for his early morning walk, had argued with a porcupine.

"Best thing we can do is get him back to Mrs. Liversedge. She's as good as a vet, they say. And she'll be worrying about him."

As she escorted her father, carefully carrying his precious bundle, Karen was conscious of a deep feeling of relief. Dogo was safe, though injured, and no one could blame a leopard for his misfortunes. Whatever had menaced the boys from the trees that morning was an actor in another play, not the villain in the tragedy of Dogo. And, just for a change, Ajax was a hero, instead of a culprit.

Mrs. Liversedge certainly thought so. She found time, among her gruff shouts of joy and exclamations of horror, to biff Ajax on his broad back and

tell him he was a "dashed good scout." Mrs. Liversedge went one better.

"Those pups of yours. This chap the father?"

Karen nodded.

"Then you can put me down for one. If they
aren't all booked. Good stock. Give Dogo a play-
mate." And she switched to Swahili and kept her
house servant, Sabuni, dashing to and fro with hot
water and clean rags and medicated ointment.

Karen was delighted. This was just what she had
hoped for, a puppy living close at hand that she
would be able to watch grow up.

After this further excitement, the Elliott household was able to settle down. Joshua went off to his
house for his free Saturday afternoon, and was soon
seen in his best suit, wending his way down the
drive with his wife and family trailing behind him,
umbrellas held high. Mungai disappeared on his
bicycle, draped in polythene to protect his tropical-
white Salvation Army uniform. Mungai played the
drum in the band at the Salvation Army meeting
up at the shopping center each Saturday. (Karen
sometimes went along to join in the hymn singing.)

Mrs. Elliott creamed the butter and sugar for a
cake for tea and sang as she worked, pleased to
have her kitchen to herself. Jenny took her afternoon nap, and Mr. Elliott returned to his magazine
and daydreamed of coffee plantations. Karen
groomed the dogs and fed Tina with vitamin pills.
Then, rewarding herself for virtue, she played with
the puppies until the visitors were due.

Richard and his friends arrived at four o'clock,

unusually neat and tidy. They were all pleased to hear that Dogo had been found, and Ajax came in for some more compliments.

"We must try him at tracking," said Richard, rubbing Ajax under his chin. "Give him an old sock of Jock's and turn him loose. He'd probably lead us straight to the nearest baboon troop."

"Oh yeah?" said Jock, and Karen hastily turned the conversation.

"Did I ever show you this?" she asked, and she led the three boys over to the old-fashioned radio which stood on a small table against the far wall. Karen gently turned the set around. Because it was old, the back had warped and did not fit closely. A tuft of grubby white wool protruded from a hole at the base. Karen eased the back panel outwards and stood aside so that Richard could peer into the radio. Odds and ends of fluff and fabric were heaped in one corner beneath the valves. Richard poked the mound cautiously and it stirred beneath his finger. A small gray head emerged suddenly from the top. Eyes goggled at them. Then there was a flurry and a tiny form, more tail than torso, shot past them, tobogganed down the table leg, and darted away under an armchair.

"Why, it's a dormouse!" said Richard.

"Is it?" said Karen. "I did wonder. I knew it wasn't a mouse because of that fluffy tail."

"Going to make a pet of it?" asked Richard.

"Oh no, I think it's more fun as it is. The dogs don't seem to take any notice of it, even though it sometimes runs right under their sleepy old noses. Look at Ajax this minute!"

Ajax dozed on the floor. He had not stirred when the dormouse fled past him. Even Angus was interested in the dormouse and the ice was broken. The conversation turned to the odd places animals chose to nest in. Every Kenya dweller could hold forth on that subject.

When tea was ready the dogs were shut in the dining room, and for a while the room was quiet while everyone munched and drank. Then cups and plates were stacked back on the tea trolley and mouths were free once more for conversation.

"Are you busy tomorrow, Karen?" asked Richard. "Dad's on duty in the game park in the afternoon, and he says he'll take us with him. You too, if you like." During the rains visitors to the game park often become bogged down in the mud, and members of the staff drove around on the lookout for casualties. "He'll be down by the stream where the lions have been all week. There's sure to be a crowd down there."

"Oh super," said Karen. "May I go, Mummy?" Her mother nodded. She was busy removing chocolate cake from Jenny's nose, ears and forehead.

"Talking of lions," said Angus suddenly. "Did Karen tell you about the leopard this morning, Mr. Elliott?"

Karen's father had been sitting quietly in a corner. He looked up sharply. "No? Why, what happened? Karen didn't say a word."

"We were in that overgrown plot across the road,

where the empty house is. Hunting for Dogo. And Ajax stopped dead. Wouldn't budge. And he started growling. We all felt a bit nervous, so we retreated, and something coughed at us as we went, a nasty snarly sort of cough. Richard thought it was a leopard."

"It was," said Richard.

"Panic, that's what we felt," said Angus thoughtfully. "Panic-fear. Fear of the great god Pan. Very interesting."

"Fear of the bloomin' leopard," said Jock.

"If it was." And Karen scowled at a praying mantis that was worshiping on the windowsill.

"Well, it was. I bet it was," said Richard, taking up the challenge. "It probably lives in there. I told Dad and he said that one of the poultry farms not far from here has been bothered by a leopard for some time. Yes, and what's more, John Matuki—you know, Dad's friend in the Game Department who lives in Langata himself—has talked them into letting him have a go at trapping it. They were going to try to shoot it, of course."

"Shoot it?"

"Well, wouldn't you, if a leopard got in and killed half your stock?"

"We must keep a close eye on the dogs," said Mr. Elliott. "And Karen, don't you just wander off. Stick to birdwatching at home for a while."

That reminded Karen of something. And she wanted to change the subject. "Richard, remember you promised to help me build a blind down by the

murram pit? I saw a heron down there last week.
Could we do it now? Soon, anyway. OK?"

Richard looked across at Angus, who raised one
eyebrow. "Well, if I've got time, Karen. Angus and
I have plans."

"But you promised, ages ago! That's not fair,"
said Karen.

"Get Jock to help you," said Richard. "Do him
good. Get his weight down."

Karen made no answer. She bent her head to hide
her sulky mouth and plaited her fingers. Why did
Angus have to come and spoil things?

"Could we go and see the puppies?" asked Jock
at that moment. It was a popular suggestion. There
was a general move toward the door. Puppies were
consoling things. Karen hugged Honey Bear and
forgot, for the moment, about leopards and boys
and the difficulties of life.

Later that evening, after the boys had gone home,
Mr. Elliott and Mungai met to see what could be
done with the smoke bomb. The rain had stopped,
and the clouds had parted sufficiently to show a
half-grown moon sailing across the sky behind the
slender outlines of the gum trees.

Karen, soaking comfortably in a hot bath with a
bird book propped up on the soap tray near her
chin, heard the soft footsteps outside and guessed
what was happening. She went on with her reading
until her mother banged on the door and ordered
her out. She was vigorously toweling her shoulders
when the buzzing started. Evidently there had been
survivors of the ant raid that morning.

The furious buzzing noise grew stronger and stronger, until Karen wondered that the angry bees did not burst through the ceiling into the bathroom. She did not like to think of their second struggle for life and she hastily finished drying and fled to the sitting room in her striped pajamas to report to her parents. By the time she returned to brush her teeth, the buzzing was fading away.

"Well, that could mean anything," pondered Mrs. Elliott. "The smoke may have sent them all to sleep, or the bees may have swarmed, or it may have been a complete failure and the bees have now calmed down and are laughing at us. We'll just have to wait and see." She tucked the sheet carefully round her daughter and kissed her smooth cheek. "Good night, my love, sleep well. Tomorrow's Easter Sunday. Let's hope we have a fine day for it."

9

Leopard's-eye View

It was Easter Sunday.

The leopardess lay on a rock near her escarpment lair, toasting herself in the morning sunshine. Her golden fur glowed with a warmth and a light of its own. Below her lay the western corner of the game park, and she watched, with narrow lazy eyes, the movements of the herds of grazing animals, ant-small, as they nibbled contentedly at the needle-fine shoots of new grass. Cloud shadows sped across the plains like stampeding buffalo, and away to the right the Ngong Hills huddled under a quilt of cumulo-nimbus. More rain was on its way.

A week of relentless rain had greatly changed the look of the land. The arid stretches of sun-scorched grass, blotched with fire-blackened stubble and fuzzy with dust, were gone. Now the air was washed clean and sweet and, instead of the hot shades of sulphur and saffron, umber, ochre and mustard yellow, the plains were tinted green, the cool mouth-watering shades of lime and lettuce, apple, mint and avocado. Paperflowers littered the turf.

The leopardess flexed her paws, rasping each claw lovingly against the hard rock. She patted at a basking lizard, which skittered away in a panic, leaving its tail beneath her paw. This she poked half-heartedly, trying to provoke it to movement. Then she yawned, showing the pink cavern of her mouth, and rolled limply over onto her back, paws dangling, so that the creamy fur of her chest and belly caught the warmth of the sun. She had eaten well; her hard night's work was done. She drowsed, replete, content. Her mind purred.

She lay so still that a vulture dropped down out of the seemingly empty sky to perch on a rock nearby and inspect her with one beady eye. The leopardess kept her own eyes closed but her nostrils flared, and the tip of her tail twitched ominously. The vulture left.

But the creatures of the plain, the animals of the day, were wide awake and busy about their affairs. The grass-eaters, whose lives during recent months had depended on their ability to trek each day a little further from water hole to grazing, and back again, now luxuriated in the abundance about them. And here and there, among the sleek adult bodies, a small form showed.

Baby zebras, freshly painted, nuzzled their placid mothers. Miniature wildebeests, black faces a shade less mournful in youth than they would be in age, kicked up their heels for the joy of living in a pale green world, and swished their fly-whisk tails. Small kongonis, with soft eyes not yet trained to caution by fear of stalking lion and hunting dog, peered out from behind their parents and bleated to each other.

To the southeast, the land rose steadily and was thickly wooded. Crotons, muhugus, eucalyptus, Kenya olive and Cape chestnut trees grew in profusion. At the edge of this forest, if the leopardess had cared to look, a strange scene was taking place. Two male giraffes stood shoulder to shoulder, swinging their flexible necks and striking at each other with their rudimentary horns. The whack and smack of neck on neck came startlingly clear through the quiet of the morning. Around the duelists a semicircle of giraffes stood watching with critical attention.

Not far from the giraffes, below the forest, there ran a track, and near the track there was a water hole. Here herons stood like one-legged sentinels among the reeds and bulrushes, and unwary frogs made tiny circular ripples on the glistening surface of the water. Sacred ibis searched the mud for food, their heads and curving bills sharply black, and their white plumage clean against the brown of the earth. Egrets, like exotic white flowers, trimmed the branches of a fever tree, and a darter perched on a log, its snakelike neck held ready to strike as it watched for fish.

There was a sudden commotion near the water hole. With an indignant squawk, a crowned crane shot three feet into the air, flapping heavy black-fringed wings, and landed a short distance away. There was a rustle among the reeds and a face peered out, a catlike face with rounded ears, colored gold and black, so like the leopardess—and yet not like. The face lacked menace. The fur was door-mat-harsh, and two black lines swept down from eyes to mouth in the curve of a mandarin's moustache. The slanted eyes danced. This was a cheetah.

The crane, shaking her golden crest, tilted her head to one side and continued through the reeds, hunting for frogs. Behind her, to the left this time, there came again a betraying rustle. Whoops—once again the crane hoisted herself into the air, feathers ruffled, long legs dangling, her squawk startling the egrets into flight. A second cat face showed among the reeds.

Twice more the crane erupted from the reeds and twice more she settled back, smoothing her petticoats, to stalk with an air of nervous hauteur between the stems of papyrus growing at the far side of the pool. The tall stalks with their tasseled heads echoed the slender neck and graceful crest of the crane. The cheetahs chivied her along with short bursts of speed, their greyhound legs carrying them lightly over the reed clumps, but they made no attempt to catch her and it was obvious that the crane knew this. She, in her turn, made no attempt to fly away from the water hole, but merely squawked and flapped at each interruption like an elderly spinster bothered by a wasp.

Tiring finally of the game, the cheetahs left the reeds and bounded away across the plains, stopping now and then to look about them with intelligent eyes, as if in search of further mischief. A second crane flew up to join the first.

Toward midday the clouds closed in, shutting out the sun and sponging the color from the game park scene. A sudden downpour scattered the animals, some sheltering under the nearest tree while others stood, their backs to the storm, hides streaming water, enduring stoically and chewing still at the sweet young grass beneath their dripping hoofs.

The leopardess had long since taken refuge in the cave she had made her lair. Here she slept, dry and snug, with only an occasional twitch or quiver to hint at the dreams which visited her in her sleep.

The rain ceased, but the day remained cool and gray. The leopardess stayed where she was, and few sounds penetrated her fastness—the caw of a crow, the mew of a hovering kite, the harsh scolding of a fiscal shrike high on the escarpment. When, later in the afternoon, the Land Rover passed along the track far, far beneath her, the noise of the engine did not reach her.

And Karen, seated in the front seat next to Jock Duncan and Mr. Faulkner, did not look up. She kept her eyes on the plains.

10

A Variety of Cats

It was always a treat for Karen to go to the game park with Mr. Faulkner. He was not a talkative man, but when he did talk he had something to say, and Karen treasured his stories about animals and the setting up of the game parks and the last-ditch efforts of men to preserve what they had come so near to destroying—the fantastic wildlife of East Africa.

He was talking now about conservation, half to the children, half to himself. Karen sat, joggling against Jock, as the Land Rover left the forest area and swung around onto the track which skirted the plains. Jock was a bulky companion on the narrow seat. "Good job I'm skinny," thought Karen.

"Take leopards," said Mr. Faulkner. "Some animals can't be fenced in, and the leopard is one.

That means he invades territory man has earmarked for his own, and preys on man's property. The average farmer has just one reaction—kill. Get rid of the pest. And how can you blame him? A man spends his life building up a herd of cattle, or running a poultry farm, and a wild animal comes along and ruins him in one night.

"But it isn't always that simple. It's much easier to shoot a leopard, for instance, than it is to keep down the numbers of baboons and other monkeys. Leopards do a far more efficient job on baboons than man does—their mere presence in a district keeps the baboons on the move. So, kill the leopards and what do you get? Farms and African *shambas* overrun by baboons, maize fields raided, crops destroyed, and a great deal of money, time and temper spent trying to cope with 'em.

"Leopards are crafty animals, and one of the last to leave built-up areas. They can conceal themselves in places you wouldn't think good enough to hide a rabbit. Like this one of Richard's, if it *was* a leopard—OK, OK, I think you're probably right —they turn up unexpectedly. What we try to do, when we can, is trap the beast and cart him off somewhere where he won't be in man's way." And Mr. Faulkner fell silent, sighing inwardly as he thought of the numbers of animals slaughtered each year because, it seemed, there was no room for them, and man, in the same world.

A family of ostriches strutted toward them, drab mother in the lead, followed by a dozen half-grown chicks, turkey-sized.

"Plain janes, the lot of 'em," said Richard, looking them over with a practiced eye. "They take after Mum."

"Oh, they're just at the awkward stage, teen-age, all legs and nose—like you and Angus," said Karen. Jock snorted, and Richard pulled her ponytail from the back seat.

They were heading for a spot some miles away where a row of fever trees marked the course of a stream. This was a favorite spot for lions who often lay up in the bushes or under the trees during the day and it was here that visitors came in search of them. When a dozen or so cars maneuvered for position in a small muddy area of ground pitted with ant-bear and warthog holes, there was usually trouble.

They were driving now past a water hole rimmed with reeds and bulrushes. Two crowned cranes calmly hunted frogs as if nothing on earth could disturb their dignity. A doe impala stepped out of the rushes, twin fawns at her heels. The babies stared wide-eyed at the Land Rover, ears startled. Then the little group leaped away to safety on their long fragile legs, tails twitching anxiously from side to side.

Further on they passed a salt lick where several giraffes, their forelegs impossibly far apart, were enjoying the salt, while others kept watch. All around were family parties of zebra, wildebeest and hartebeest.

Then the track forked, and Mr. Faulkner drove off across the plains. Here the earth changed from red coffee soil to black cotton soil, water collected in pools along the tire ruts, and the mud was deep and clinging.

Soon there came an interruption. A troop of baboons were scattered over the grass and along the track, feeding, feuding and having fun. One large dog baboon was standing sentry on top of a stump by the side of the road.

Wham! As the Land Rover drove by, the baboon leaped and thumped down on the bonnet. He took a firm grip on the windshield wipers and pressed his gaunt face against the glass. Karen squeaked, and the boys laughed and made faces at the monkey.

"Not again!" Mr. Faulkner set the Land Rover jouncing from side to side of the track. "I've met this boy before. He's car crazy and sits waiting all day to thumb a ride. Baboons often chase after cars for food, but this one just wants a lift, and he won't get off till he feels like it. The tourists egg him on, but one day he'll bite somebody, or damage a car, and then there'll be trouble. Never trust a baboon, Karen, they've no manners. It's just smash and grab with them."

Karen felt guilty; she too had fed car-hopping baboons. They put on speed, but the baboon clung on and leered at them through the windshield. Finally, as if he had reached his bus stop, he vaulted to the ground; and, as they drove away, they could see him sitting by the side of the track, waiting for the next car coming in the opposite direction to take him back to his troop.

Then they arrived. Just as Mr. Faulkner had expected, there was a semicircle of cars on a stretch of grass near the stream, where the ground sloped steeply. Three acacias, sad-looking trees with sage-green leaves and trunks of sulphur-yellow, grew near the bank in a tangle of bushes. Five lions, one male and four females, lay among the damp grass under the bushes, limp tawny bodies blending with their surroundings.

More cars were approaching. Mr. Faulkner parked his Land Rover well back from the scene so that he could keep an eye on all aspects. He stuffed tobacco into the smoky yellow bowl of his Tanganyika meerschaum pipe with practiced fingers. Then, the pipe satisfactorily lit, he slumped in his seat and gazed thoughtfully through the windshield. The children settled down for a long wait.

Although the rain was holding off, the afternoon was dull and chilly. On fine holiday afternoons, when crowds of visitors competed to find the best spot to view lions, there was sometimes trouble of a different kind. If the lions were too sleepy, too "tame," foolish people tried to stir them up. Tourists with movie cameras expected action, and men showed off before their womenfolk. More than once Mr. Faulkner had stopped visitors from throwing coins and stones at the lions to rouse them. He had gently but firmly persuaded amateur photographers not to sit on the roofs of their cars to take close-ups, nor to wander over toward a playful group of cubs in search of the best light. The lions were so used to cars that they ignored them,

but they were in no way tamed. They would make short work of the visitor who presumed too far.

When Karen had arrived in Nairobi she had been thrilled and delighted by her early glimpses of lions playing in the sun like giant pussycats. Her first view of a kill, however, had brought home to her the other side of the picture. One did not take liberties with a lion.

While Mr. Faulkner brooded on the iniquities of tourists (he much preferred lions), the children lion-watched and bird-spotted and talked among themselves. Karen reported on the bee situation; there had been no sign of life from the nest that day. And a family of jackal pups popped in and out of

their multi-passaged home beneath a nearby hillock
and watched the lion-watchers.

It seemed that the lions were hungry. As the unseen sun sank low, and the light faded, they roused
from their slumbers to stand with heads lifted and
nostrils distended, sifting the wind for betraying
scents. They moved off, heavy and intent, through
the row of glossy, mud-splashed cars. The meeting
broke up.

One by one the drivers started their engines. They
edged their way up the slope and back onto the
track. Some lurched and skidded, some crashed
their gears and stalled and slipped, but soon all
save one were on their way, leaving the park to the

lions and leopards, the zebra and wildebeest, the cool night winds and the chill driving rain.

The last car was small and old. All around it the ground lay churned up like a plowed field, black and greasy. The little car struggled and strove, moving forward and sliding back into one deep slimy rut, wheels spinning. The watching children saw a window go down, and saw the driver's features sag with dismay as she realized the fix she was in. They saw the startled glance at the fast disappearing tail-lights of the other cars heading for Nairobi and civilization, a glance which took in the growing gloom around trees and bush, while the first jackal of the evening appeared by the stream and owls with blunt shadows flitted silently over the plain.

Mr. Faulkner went into action. The Land Rover moved forward purposefully, jolting over stones and earth mounds. It was the work of a few moments for him, with Richard's help, to fix a towrope to the stranded car's bumper. While a hyena watched them with interest he drove off carefully, and the muddy little car came out of its bed with a soft glugging noise and followed dutifully behind the Land Rover.

"Big Brother to all the world, even tourists. That's Dad," said Richard cheerfully. He wiped mud from his hands onto a rag.

They established the other car on a reasonably firm track and escorted it toward the entrance. At the gate Mr. Faulkner met a friend, a man from up-country paying a brief visit to Nairobi. There was news to exchange, tales to tell, and time slipped by. It was quite dark by the time they left the game park and headed for home, and by that time it was raining once more. The children huddled in the Land Rover, while the rain thrummed on the roof with impatient fingers. Outside all was cold and wet and wild; inside it was warm and cosy and safe. They felt drowsy and content, and there was little conversation. Angus and Richard checked over a list of birds, while Jock picked at a scab on his knee and wondered what was for supper; toasted cheese would go down well. Karen daydreamed. (There she was, the only woman game warden in Kenya. . . .)

The rain danced in the headlights as they picked up speed and swarming termites mashed themselves against the windshield, leaving greasy splotches which lowered visibility still further. Karen pressed her nose against the window and watched the frogs playing "last across" as they leaped from puddle to puddle on the road. At last they neared home. The rain was slackening to a fine drizzle.

"I'll drop you off first, Karen," said Mr. Faulkner, as he slowed to take the bend. He entered the driveway, and then headlights lit up a large form standing quite still in the middle of the path.

"Botheration, Ajax is out . . ." began Karen. She stopped.

"Not Ajax this time," said Mr. Faulkner softly, his foot on the brake. "Watch him crouch and now, see how he turns his head." One eye gleamed green in the headlight. "That's a leopard, Karen. Hyenas tend to shift their gaze, while a lion glares back with both eyes."

The leopard half stood, half crouched, in a halo of light. For a moment no one spoke. Then:

"Coo lummy, what a whopper," whispered Jock. "He'd make two of the dogs. Think that's what snarled at us yesterday?"

"Indubitably," said Angus.

"Hoo!" said Jock, not liking the thought.

"What's the matter with his coat, Dad? He looks a bit battered, doesn't he? And his ear's torn."

"Yes, he's been fighting, I should think. And he's big, even for a male. A tough customer."

"A male?" asked Karen. She had been keeping very quiet.

"Well, yes, Karen, what do you think? The females don't run that size."

"Oh," said Karen. Her dream leopard had, from the first, been a female. And not a tough customer. And not battered.

"Why doesn't he make for cover?" asked Angus.

"I think we'll hurry him a little." Mr. Faulkner dipped his headlights once or twice, then sounded his horn. The leopard straightened up. It turned its head and glared fully at the intruding car, and the children could see the scarred face and swollen eye. Then, with offhand grace, it padded across the drive and leaped silently away over a flower bed into the masking darkness.

"Keep an eye on Ajax and Tina this evening, Karen," said Mr. Faulkner.

Karen blinked at him. "Would a leopard attack a big dog?" she asked. "A dog the size of an Alsatian?"

"Might think twice about old Ajax, but Tina's not so very large, is she?" said Richard.

"Best to be on the safe side," said Mr. Faulkner. He drove on. "Tell your father about the leopard, won't you, Karen?" he added, as Karen climbed down from the Land Rover. She looked up and met his eyes. She sometimes felt Mr. Faulkner could read her thoughts.

"Yes, yes, of course I will," she promised, and dived for the house.

Karen kept her word, but she stayed quiet while her parents discussed the leopard. Two leopards, she puzzled. Could there be two? Surely her leopard, the first leopard, had not been so large, so heavily built, so brutal about head and shoulders as the one seen that night.

She lay on the rug after supper, cuddling Honey Bear, with Tina at her side and Ajax, dry and well-groomed and smelling delicately of new woolen blanket, close at hand. She watched his strong white teeth as he chewed at a small stone stuck between his toes, and he sat up and grinned at her with his black clown's mouth.

"Ajax has got a tick," she said, and reached forward to pluck a bulging blob from his velvet ear.

"They were both smothered with them," sighed her mother. "Did I miss one? I picked dozens of tiny new ones off them this afternoon, when I brushed them. They must have been in the cow meadows. Where are you going to put that one, Karen?" she asked suddenly. "Not in my coffee cup!"

"You've finished, haven't you?" asked Karen, on the defensive. She yawned, rolled over, plopped the puppy down on Tina, and got to her feet. "OK, don't fuss, I'll put it outside," she promised.

She wandered out through the kitchen and dropped the tick into a watering can outside the back door. Far away a hyena whooped and wailed. Close at hand a barn owl hooted. Karen stood, staring out into the night. Where was the leopard now? What was it doing?

"I wonder . . ." said Karen.

11

A Night of Surprises

All was not well with the eagle owl. Intruders had driven him from his favorite perch in his favorite tree. He sat, a huddle of feathers, at the top of a tall muhugu, and he hooted lugubriously—*hu-hu—hu-hu-hu—ho-ho*.

The poultry too, on Jensen's farm, were unsettled. There had been considerable human activity that afternoon and, disturbed by comings and goings, hammerings and thumpings, the chickens, ducks and turkeys remained alert even with the coming of the night. Cluckings, quacks and gobbles came in waves from shed after shed, one group setting off another, but gradually the birds quietened until only an occasional squawk broke the silence and blended with the hooting of the eagle owl.

Then came the night visitors. Under the cover of

the surrounding darkness, and unchecked by the dim lights left burning among the sheds, many hopeful predators came regularly to check the gates and test the wire mesh which roofed as well as walled the hen runs. Some tried to dig an entrance; others merely sniffed greedily at the scent of feathered food so near, yet so exasperatingly out of reach.

The first arrival on the scene was a small slinky animal whose black fur coat, striped with white, and long tail seemed to invite attention. But more powerful creatures—jackal or genet—meeting him on his journeyings, stepped aside to let him pass. The zorilla, sometimes called the African skunk, had a noisome reputation.

The zorilla was after eggs, or chicks. But all seemed bolted and barred and he shuffled off after a casual inspection. The night was young, the poultry farm his first port of call.

The pair of silver-backed jackals who came next were far more persistent. There was one place in particular that seemed to draw them back time and again. This was a small shed, or large box, and was new to the jackals, who were regular poultry farm visitors. The jackals sniffed eagerly around it, edging each other aside but never quite venturing up to the entrance. For this box, it seemed, had no door and there was something inside with an enticing smell. But the newness was disturbing. And so were other smells which clung to the box despite the heavy rain of early evening. They might, how-

ever, have plucked up courage to enter if an odd—
and terrifying—thing had not happened.

Out of the darkness, and down from the sky, a
rock thudded, missing the male jackal by inches
and sending him and his wife fleeing from the scene.
From somewhere nearby, disembodied, there came
a quiet chuckle.

Hours passed. The moon appeared among the
drifting clouds. Frogs made background music from
their puddles. A porcupine appeared and rattled
toward the vegetable garden. A mongoose slid among
the sheds. The dispossessed eagle owl protested
mournfully—*hu-hu*—*hu-hu-hu*—*ho-ho*—from his
muhugu tree. The roosting birds twitched in their
sleep and huddled closer together.

Then all at once the night noises switched themselves off. There came a period of silence—strained,
waiting, frightened silence.

And the male leopard padded down the line of
poultry sheds.

The smell of blood hung in the air, warm and
sticky sweet. The leopard was aware of it with
every nerve of his powerful body. But there were
other smells.

He circled warily round the box, which stood at
the end of a row of poultry houses. It was his first
visit to this particular poultry farm and he had investigated each house in turn. Each smelled ex-
citingly of feathers and fear. He coughed, low in
his throat, moved nervously, coughed again as he
approached the opening in the box. His claws ex-

tended, retracted, scoring the soft damp earth. His tail moved behind him with a life of its own.

He had eaten nothing since dawn on Saturday, and the smell of blood was in his brain. It swirled crimson before his eyes, blurring his vision, marring his judgment. But with the smell of blood there came the smell of man.

Nothing stirred within the box. Nothing cackled, fluttered, scrabbled, or by retreating urged him on, spurring his lust to rend and tear, to kill. His hunger stirred inside him, rose in his throat, dripped from his open mouth. But still the cold forbidding smell of human sweat barred him from the entrance to the box.

The leopard moved away. He prowled restlessly once more around the hen runs, rubbed his heavy sides against fence posts, pressed on wire mesh, clawed at gateways. There was no way in. The smell of man was here too but blurred, swamped by the smell of life, of fusty feathers, droppings, sour vegetation.

He was stiff and sore from his wounds. His swollen eye throbbed. He needed food. He returned to the box. To the smell of fresh blood. To the smell of death that meant the end of hunger.

He entered, walking on cautious velvet paws, claws sheathed. The sides of the box pressed ominously down on him, and he snarled, panicked in his turn; and the sound echoed, adding to the leopard's fear and reaching other listening ears not far away.

Two dead chickens lay crumpled against the back

of the box, necks awry. The leopard nuzzled one, thrusting his blunt scarred muzzle deep into the limp softness. He was still wary, still on guard. He arched his thick neck and snarled a challenge at the menace of the walls. Then hunger took possession of his mind, and he seized a chicken in his murderous mouth, tossing it from side to side like a terrier killing a rat, so that the dead head flapped against his shoulders in futile protest. He began to eat.

And, as he did so, a metal grid crashed down across the entrance to the box.

The trap was sprung.

Thus it was that when, later that night, the leopardess in her turn explored the poultry farm, she found neither food nor trap, only a cage filled with anger. The leopard still raged. He clawed at the grid as she approached, and spat at her, and she turned and leaped away, filled with fear.

The eagle owl hooted, as if in mockery.

12

Leopard Cliffs

It was Richard who brought the news, two days later, on the Tuesday morning.

He arrived on the doorstep immediately after breakfast.

"*Jambo,* everyone," he said, and gave Karen a wink. "What d'you think? Remember I told you the game department was laying a trap for a leopard on Jensen's poultry farm? Yep, well, they caught one. On Sunday night! What d'you bet it was the one we saw on your drive? Dad heard yesterday and we drove round with John Matuku to have a decko. John perched up a tree half Sunday night until they had the leopard in the bag. He's a huge brute—the leopard, I mean. And boy, is he in a mess. Something's scratched him to pieces. So John says they'll keep him for a few days and try to get some *dawa* into him—penicillin or something. Though I'm blowed if I know how you give a leopard an injection," he added thoughtfully. "But anyhow, John says they'll release it in the park at the end of the week, very early one morning, and Dad says—listen, Karen—that he'll take us all to watch!"

Richard paused for breath and absently helped himself to a stray slice of toast.

"Oh, Richard, me too?" Karen flung herself at him from across the room and hugged him tightly round the neck. Then, flushing vividly, she let go and turned to her mother.

"May I go, Mummy, please, may I?"

"Why yes, of course you can go, Karen, if Mr. Faulkner can put up with you. It's very kind of him to let you tag along. Don't you get in the way, though, or be silly. And do just what he tells you!"

"Gosh, Richard, thank you. I'm thrilled to bits," said Karen, her eyes bright. "Is Jock excited?"

"Well, he didn't hug me, if that's what you mean!" said Richard pointedly, straightening his collar. He reached for the butter dish and buttered his toast lavishly. He took a bite. "Ah, toothmarks," he said, regarding the toast with satisfaction. "Only way to tell if you've got enough butter."

When Richard had gone, Karen wandered into the sitting room. Her mind was in a whirl. She sat cross-legged on the rug with Ajax and stared out of the French windows at the rain dripping off the veranda roof and the lawn grass "visibly growing," as her mother said. If, thought Karen. If the leopard, her leopard, had been trapped, but was safe and would be released to live once more in freedom, this was good. There would be no more chance encounters, and these had added a pinch of the spice of excitement to the past ten days. But she knew they were dangerous, especially for the dogs. But was this her leopard? "A huge brute," Richard had said and, yes, this description fitted the leopard they had met on the drive. But she still could not reconcile her memory-picture of the leopard in the tree with the reality of this latest meeting. Her leopard had been golden, feline, beautiful, feminine—and frightening. But not huge. And not a brute. Oh well, she would see the leopard again, more closely, on the release day, and try to fit the puzzle pieces together.

Karen fussed and fidgeted through the next few days, and her fingernails suffered; but eventually the time passed. If the rain held off the leopard was to be released shortly after dawn on Friday, when it was unlikely there would be any visitors about.

"Won't the leopard find his way back, Mr. Faulkner?" asked Karen that morning. She and the boys were seated in the Land Rover, feeling hollow with excitement and lack of breakfast, while ahead of them a big truck nosed its way cautiously down a muddy game park track. A tarpaulin-covered crate was lashed to the back of the truck, which John Matuku was driving. With John rode a green-capped game ranger, Amram by name.

"It's about fifteen miles, Karen. We're going to let him go at the edge of Leopard Cliffs, where he'll feel at home and where there should be plenty of game. Any other time of year we'd send him down to Tsavo, but the Mombasa Road is flooded so we're trying it this way. I hope it works, because he's already found a way in among the chickens once, and he'll keep trying. David Jensen will be out shooting game wardens as well as leopards if he has any more trouble."

"They go berserk when they kill, don't they, Mr. Faulkner?" said Jock cheerfully. He was chewing toffee to deaden his hunger pangs and his round cheeks bulged more than ever. "Sort of kill for the fun of it?"

"Some people say so, Jock. But the leopard is one of the few wild animals that makes provision for the future. Have you ever seen a leopard's larder? I know you have, Richard. Sometimes in the forest you'll see a dead gazelle or half-eaten dik-dik stashed high in the fork of a tree, out of reach of hyenas. You can guess a leopard did that. Funny thing—the vultures leave it alone. And some naturalists have come to think that when a leopard kills half the sheep in a sheep run, or dozens of hens, far more than he can possibly eat, it's because of this instinct he has to stockpile. And of course you have to allow for the excitement he feels at being penned in with frantic animals. He doesn't get much chance to kill like that in the wilds. The creatures are not shut in; by the time he's caught one the others are escaping.

"The leopard is a fascinating beast—to me, anyhow. They have nothing much to fear but the man with the gun. Unfortunately that is the fate they usually meet—killed as a pest, or for their fur coats. By the way, did you ever hear that what probably saved man, in the days when he was weak and predators were larger, was that he not only smells nasty but he tastes nasty? Animals don't eat us, kids, because they don't like us!"

A thought had struck Karen. "Do leopards hunt in pairs, Mr. Faulkner? Do they stick together?"

"No, Karen. They're too jealous of each other, unlike lions who work together when they're hunting, and have an interesting family life. The leopard is an individual, kith and kin to the Cat that Walked by Himself."

"What about when they have cubs?"

"The female rears them by herself, and she trains them to hunt. There are usually only two or three to a litter, and often only one, the strongest, survives."

"Oh," said Karen, saying good-by to her latest theory.

The day had dawned bright, following the pattern. In the spanking clean air of early morning every blade of grass gleamed, every pool sparkled, as if Nature were a proud housewife. Birds sang in the thickets of wait-a-bit thorn and across the plain a herd of zebra galloped toward a water hole.

Leopard Cliffs, where the leopard was to be released, was the name given to one side of a deep gorge, rocky and thickly treed, where visitors to the park were allowed to leave their cars and walk to the cliff edge for the sake of the view, and to spot the shyer, more wary animals that stayed within its shelter.

For some distance they retraced the journey they had made on Sunday, toward the lions' resting place. Then they swung off to the south. Karen looked for the car-hopping baboon, but, at that time in the morning, he was probably not expecting visitors. Some way from the track she did notice a troop of baboons scattered among the branches of a tree. They were yawning and scratching themselves in an "Oh dear, it's time to get up," sort of manner, and she guessed he was with them. Looking back, as the car turned off, she saw one baboon leap onto a post by the road and stare after them. If it was he, he had missed the bus.

"I love the park in the morning," she said shyly to Mr. Faulkner. "You can forget the town is so near and imagine yourself back in the Africa that used to be, when all the world was one big game park."

"Mmmm. No cars, no dusty roads, no petrol fumes, no cigarette packets or Coke bottles—but no us either," said Mr. Faulkner, smiling.

"No you, but lots of me," said Jock. "Trotting bravely past the lions with a spear in my right hand and a dead impala flung over my left shoulder, my muscles rippling under my glossy brown skin."

"Crawling timidly past the lions, you mean," said Angus from behind them. "With your teeth chattering in your glossy brown head."

"Sprinting for your life past the lions," said Richard. "Bent double under the weight of a dead mole rat."

"Lay off," said Jock. "Me, I'm strong. Look at my muscles!" He crooked his arm and clenched his fist.

"The muscles on his brawny arms stood out like sparrows' kneecaps," chanted a voice from the rear.

"The muscles on his brawny arms stood out like bullfrog's eyeballs," chanted the second voice.

"LAY OFF," said Jock.

"It's all very well for boys," said Karen in her gloomiest voice, following her own train of thought and ignoring the others. "The Masai morani have a smashing time; but I don't think the women do. They look old in no time. It wouldn't suit me, anyway. I'd rather be a female leopard than a female Masai."

"It's much the same in the animal world, Karen," said Mr. Faulkner, his voice solemn but laughter in his eyes. "Just think how the lazy male lion bosses the lioness, and even though she works hardest to make a kill she has to sit and wait until her lord and master has taken the edge off his appetite. I should stay civilized, if I were you. It has its compensations for a girl—even if you can't be a game warden."

Karen heaved a sigh, but ahead of them the truck had turned off the track and pulled up. She could see the trees bordering the gorge and jagged rocks gleaming white, toothlike, where the cliffs caught the sun. She brightened.

Leaving the children in the Land Rover, Mr.

Faulkner joined the other men and they set to work. A ramp was fitted to the back of the truck and the heavy crate, containing a hundred and fifty pounds of leopard, was lowered to the ground as carefully and steadily as possible. Whenever a man came into view the leopard snarled, fighting them with his eyes and bared teeth through the protecting grid. The men were careful to keep to the back and sides of the crate; a razor-clawed paw was ever ready to slash at an unwary arm or leg.

A vulture circled high overhead, gliding lazily and luxuriously, taking advantage of the warm air currents rising from the land. You could tell he was enjoying himself, thought Karen, craning her neck to watch. Free as the air, that's what it means. And even a vulture could be beautiful seen in this way. Close at hand a secretary bird came striding through the grass, red eyes alert for lizards.

The crate was down the ramp. The three men carried it a few steps to a smooth stretch of turf, close cropped by hundreds of grazing mouths. Ahead were the cliffs. To the right and left were trees and bushes. The leopard could find cover in a couple of easy bounds.

Karen felt fingers of excitement tickle her spine. The previous year she had seen a pair of lions released and everything had gone smoothly. The big cats had departed with dignity. But a leopard was different, unpredictable. Her ears winced at the snarls which rasped the air. She edged a little closer to Jock. He smelled of toffee, which was homely and comforting. Her dream bubble of a friendly golden leopard was finally pricked. Leopards were leopards. Dreams were dreams and this—this was reality.

John Matuku, a short, broad-shouldered man with blunt, cheerful features, checked the rope tied to the top of the grid. Then he and Amram returned to the truck and drove it slowly over near the Land Rover, paying out the rope. Mr. Faulkner rejoined the children, who had fallen silent and were watching big-eyed and tense.

"John will give the leopard a few moments in which to calm down," said Mr. Faulkner placidly. He thumbed tobacco into his pipe.

The minutes passed. Then—slowly, slowly—the men in the truck began to haul on the rope. There was a creak. A grating of metal on wood. Then— slowly, slowly—the grid was raised.

From the crate there came no sound, no movement. A thrush cracked a snail shell on a rock, ate his prize, and trilled his satisfaction. A bee hummed. The waiting children felt their hearts thump in their breasts and heard the faint hiss of their breath in their nostrils.

Inside, out of sight, the leopard cowered mistrustfully against the back of the crate, watching and waiting in his turn. His head swung this way, that way. His nostrils flared, his breath came fast. He sensed a trap; he scented man. Then, step by wary step, he crept toward the sunlight, his nose wild with the tantalizing scents of freedom—clover, herbs and crushed warm grass. At the edge of the crate he stopped. The grid cast a forbidding bar of shadow between planks and grass. A butterfly danced across the opening—and the leopard came out with a rush.

He wheeled. And saw the waiting cars.

Beside him was the gorge, the way of escape. But the leopard smelled the hated smell of man, thick on the crate, tainting the air. His half-healed wounds pained him as he moved, adding to his anger. His sojourn in the crate had left him stiff. The jolting journey had rubbed his temper raw. Beside him was the gorge. But the truck lay to the right, the Land Rover to the left. Nearer.

With a snarl of rage, ears flat against his head, the leopard leaped for the Land Rover.

13

Karen Faces Reality

CRASH!

The leopard's heavy body thudded down on the thin steel of the Land Rover's roof with an impact that jolted the watchers forward in their seats. Karen cried out, Jock yelped, and Mr. Faulkner's pipe jerked from his mouth and fell with a shower of sparks onto the floor.

"Watch out!" yelled John Matuku belatedly from the truck. There was a sudden roar and clatter as he started the engine and crashed the gears, but the noise from the truck was drowned by the revving of the Land Rover's own engine and the awful sounds of the clawing raging leopard immediately over their heads.

"Hold on, kids," snapped Mr. Faulkner. "I'll try to shake him off."

The Land Rover lurched forward. Normally the sound of the motors would have sent the leopard streaking for cover. In his present blind rage he merely clung tighter, snarled louder. The roof of the cab was already buckling under his weight. Karen stared upward, her face white, her heart pounding wildly. She clung to the seat with stiff cold fingers.

Mr. Faulkner bucketed the car over the rough ground, dodging trees and crashing through low bushes.

"Omigosh!" said Jock, sliding against Karen as the car swung round. The big boys in the back lay full length, holding on with fingers and toes, thudding against each other and the sides of the Land Rover.

"I hope (jolt) there aren't any (thump) antbear holes," thought Karen, breathless and battered. WHAM! went the leopard's paw against the windshield. The cab reeked with his fetid breath.

Close at hand thundered the truck, with John Matuku driving for all he was worth and Amram leaning half out of the window, brandishing his Ranger's cap at the leopard and yelling Kamba war cries.

"It's no good," gasped Mr. Faulkner, and the sweat trickled unchecked down his tanned face. "This ground's too dangerous. I'll head for the track, then get up speed."

"Hey!" Karen clutched at Mr. Faulkner's arm, reaching across Jock, as an idea hit her, and the Land Rover rocked.

"Steady, Karen, we'll be all right," he jerked out, hanging on to the steering wheel for dear life.

"No—it's just—turn north! On the track, turn north!"

"What the . . . ?" It was no time to argue. The windshield in front of them was cracked and fogged from the leopard's attacks. The roof sagged ominously. Mr. Faulkner glimpsed the bare scraped earth of the track in front of him and swung the vehicle round. The truck swerved after them. Karen caught a glimpse of Amram, a rifle in his hands, while John Matuku fought the heavy truck.

They tore down the track, stampeding a small herd of impala, and swung crazily round a bend on two wheels. The leopard clung to the roof, tearing at the edge with his teeth and lashing out furiously with his right paw.

From side to side of the track they swerved, the passengers rattling together like pebbles in a tin can. Faster and faster they went, but still the leopard raged above their heads.

"Karen? What? Where . . . ?"

"Find the baboon, Mr. Faulkner, find the baboon," screamed Karen.

Ahead of them the track branched and, as Karen's words sank in, they lurched to the right at the last moment. The Land Rover rocked dizzily but it righted itself with a bone-shaking thud and raced on. Something moved by the track ahead of them. Mr. Faulkner braked, and the car skidded sickeningly as they slowed. Then:

SPANG! The big dog baboon leaped from his

favorite stump and landed once more on the bonnet of the Land Rover. Oozing conceit it leered through the battered windscreen. Then its nose twitched and it gave a horrified glance upwards.

Karen and Jock would have given a year's pocket money for a sight of the leopard at that moment. But they had a front-row view of the baboon; Richard and Angus only glimpsed the scene. Its mouth opened in a stupified gape as it spotted its worst enemy, and its teeth chattered with fright. Then it was away, leaping and bounding on all fours for its life across the plain, with the rest of the baboon troop scattering before it, and the leopard a scant yard behind.

Mr. Faulkner stopped the Land Rover. He drew his hand slowly down his sweat-streaked face and took a deep breath. His chest heaved under the khaki bush jacket. Then he looked at the children. But they were staring out of the windows, Angus and Richard pressing forward and peering over Karen and Jock.

A hundred yards away the leopard stood, his head strained back against the weight of the dead baboon crunched in his jaws. Blood trickled from the sides of his mouth. He stared at the onlookers with iced green eyes. Then he turned and padded unhurriedly away toward the nearest trees.

They watched him go in silence.

With a bang and a clatter the truck pulled up behind them. Jock shook himself like a spaniel, and the spell was broken. While John Matuku hurled anxious questions at Mr. Faulkner, the children exchanged glances and rubbed their bruised limbs.

"That old baboon—he sort of saved our bacon, didn't he?" said Jock.

"Indubitably," said Angus. "From a fate worse than death."

"Well, may be. We don't know what would have happened," said Richard.

"What if we'd crashed?" asked Karen.

"What if?" said Richard. "We didn't, did we? Good old Dad."

"Were you scared, Jock?" asked Karen.

"Not half," said Jock.

"Me too," said Karen.

"Quivering like a jellyfish," said Richard.

"Vibrating like an invertebrate," said Angus. "Hurray for panic fear."

"Fear of the bloomin' leopard," grunted Jock.

"Amram was going to shoot the leopard," said Karen. Richard nodded gravely and reached out a hand to where his father's own rifle was clipped to the side of the Land Rover. He patted the barrel.

"It was kind of funny, really," said Jock. "Did you see the look on that baboon's face? When he saw the leopard?"

"Ha bloomin' ha," said Karen. Then she looked at Jock, and he looked at her. The color was gradually returning to their cheeks. Their mouths twitched at the corners. "Oh, well, yes, it was funny," agreed Karen. She began to laugh, and the boys joined in. The men watched them, their own faces, still showing signs of shock, gradually relaxing into grins.

Karen stopped laughing abruptly. Her eyes filled with tears. Her lips trembled uncontrollably and she turned and hid her face against the back of the seat.

"Hey, hey. It's finished. It's over. There's nothing to cry about, old lady." Mr. Faulkner reached across Jock and his warm hand closed comfortingly on Karen's heaving shoulder.

"I'm—I'm—sorry for the baboon," sobbed Karen. "Our poor old hitchhiker. He helped us." She sniffed hard, fumbled for a handkerchief, failed to find one and wiped her eyes and nose with her jacket sleeve. Then she sat up again. "I'm all right," she said. She didn't look at the boys.

John Matuku and Amram went back to the truck. They still had to return for the empty crate. The Land Rover drove home, at regulation speed now, with sober passengers on board. The scarred glass and the bent and warped roof made a lasting souvenir of their adventure.

"Have a toffee," said Jock to Karen. She took one gratefully, and the good brown-sugar flavor slid soothingly down her throat.

"You'll go down in game park history, Karen, for that bright idea of yours," said Mr. Faulkner. "I was beginning to fear I'd have to stop and let Amram take a shot at the leopard to dislodge him." And he looked grave. The last thing any game warden wants is to have to shoot an animal.

Jock was muttering to himself, and Karen, who

was fast recovering her spirits, nudged him in the ribs. "Hey, Jock, are you giving thanks to the gods?"

"No, shut up a moment, Karen. I nearly got it."

"Got what?"

"Amram's war cry. I'll have to get him to do it for me again. Mr. Faulkner, could you ask him? Or Mr. Matuku—he's Kamba, too, isn't he? Boy, would it shake my form at school if I could let rip with a Kamba war cry at the next rugger match."

"Oh Jock," said Karen scornfully. "We've just been mauled by a man-eating leopard, or nearly man-eating, and you talk about war cries! Boys!"

"Well, if that's the last we hear of the leopard, he certainly made an impression before he went," said Richard, glancing at the roof. "With all that *matata* going on, he must have had so much to think about that Jensen's poultry farm will have faded from his memory. We hope. Anyway, *kwa heri,* leopard!"

"So long, farewell, bye-bye," said Jock. "And good riddance."

"I wonder," said Karen, but she said it so quietly that no one heard.

After so much excitement it was difficult to settle down again to ordinary holiday activities. The rains set in with a vengeance, and the children were confined to their houses. Richard and Angus read book after book on mountaineering and gazed longingly at the Ngong Hills, veiled by rain. Finally Richard started a craze for chemistry and he and Angus commandeered a spare bathroom, carried out a series of experiments, and stank the house out. Jock and Karen were not welcomed.

"Get hence, plaguey round boy," said Angus to Jock.

"Buzz off, mosquito," said Richard to Karen. He grinned as he said it, but her feelings were badly hurt.

After that Jock did what he called "pottering," which meant he got in everyone else's way. Karen stayed at home.

She was depressed. The savagery of the attack by the leopard, the close-up of the violent death of the baboon, had made a deep impression on her. She still could not make up her mind whether there had been one leopard or two. If the leopard had been in a fight, that might account for the differences which puzzled her. But she no longer had any illusions about their capacity for savagery. Her dream bubble was pricked once and for all, and briefly she shrank from thinking about leopards. But this did not last. Her love of animals went too deep. She found she did not need to romanticize them but could accept them for what they were: not good and bad, but herbivores and carnivores, grass-eaters and meat-eaters, hunted and hunters.

She began to read all she could find on leopards at the library, though this was surprisingly little, and tried to picture in her mind the life they led, until she felt she could follow them through each step of their day.

"All right," said Karen to herself. "Leopards are leopards. They're not tabby cats. *Chui*"—she savored the Swahili name—"*Chui*. Fierce or not fierce, I like them. They're beautiful—and they're interesting."

While she was still sorting out her feelings over the leopards, Karen had to cope with the departure of the puppies. They were now two months old, and homes had been found for them all.

("And thank goodness for that," said Mrs. Elliott. "It's not that they aren't sweet, Karen. But having the big dogs in the house all day during the rains is bad enough. Cleaning up after the pups is the limit. Next time, get Tina to plan things better.")

But Karen could not help feeling forlorn. She spent as much of the few remaining days as she could playing with the puppies and fondling them. Mrs. Liversedge had chosen Bruin, the biggest and most bearlike. He promised to grow up very much like his father. "In brain as well as looks," said Karen. She had already decided that Bruin was none too bright. Nandi Bear was the most intelligent, and Wee Bear, to compensate for his lack of bulk, had developed some tricky little ways of his own. Poley Bear was spoiled; visitors always made a fuss over him because he was so beautiful, with his white silk coat and dark eyes. Grizzly Bear she liked least. He still whined.

But Honey Bear!

"Oh, Honey Bear, I love you," said Karen umpteen times a day, holding the small woolly creature up in front of her eyes.

"Yip," said Honey Bear, trying frantically to lick the tip of Karen's nose.

Honey Bear was going to a farm on the Kinangop, fifty-odd miles away. Her new owner came for her on the Sunday, two days after the release of the leopard. She approved of the name, and promised to go on using it, which somewhat comforted Karen.

"Good-by, booful," whispered Karen in Honey Bear's ear as she hugged her for the last time and handed her over. "Honey Bear, I love you."

Then she was gone, and, within the next day or so, her brothers went also. Mrs. Liversedge and Dogo ("He's in tip-top form, thank you") marched over to fetch Bruin. Dogo was inclined to look askance at the puppy, who was already as heavy, if not as long, as the dachshund. But Bruin had no inhibitions. He rolled on his back in front of the dignified Dogo, exposing his fat little belly, and dabbed with his clumsy paws at Dogo's long disapproving nose. Dogo barked, and sniffed, and then made up his mind to adopt Bruin and teach him the Liversedge standard of manners. In no time at all they were inseparable.

But the house rang empty round Karen, minus yaps and whuffs. She and Tina roamed restlessly through room after room, both wearing, her mother said, much the same expression.

"No more furry babies," said Karen to Tina. "I know just how you feel."

14

Cubs

The cubs were born.

The lair was stuffy-warm and dark. The young leopardess lay on her side, breathing rapidly. This was her first litter. The sound of her panting dominated the cave but, beneath the heavier noise, a keen ear might have caught a second sound: the wet smack of tiny lips as the newborn cubs suckled, blind blunt faces pressed closely into the comfort of their mother's creamy fur. Sometimes unaccustomed mouths would lose the teat and the keenest of mews, the shrillest of squeaks, betrayed the instant anxiety, the frantic searching that ended, always, in success and milky contentment.

There were two cubs, one male, one female. The leopardess curved herself around them, reaching out with her moist pink tongue to lick the tiny forms. Earlier she had used first her teeth, savage teeth turned gentle, to clip the cord and help peel away the enclosing membrane, and then her tongue to wash and massage the newborn cubs to life, sending the blood circulating warmly in their veins and pumping air into their faltering lungs.

Now her action expressed her need for contact, as a human mother will fondle and enfold her baby. The leopardess licked her cubs and she purred, and her purring vibrated from rocky wall to rocky wall, charging the stale air with a feeling akin to electricity. The cubs sucked and, bellies plump with milk, fell suddenly asleep.

Soon the leopardess slept also.

Outside, the hunters and the hunted trod their nightly measure.

And the rain poured down.

15

Lull

Rain.

Rain, rain, rain.

Day after day, rain, pouring down, drenching, dousing, drowning the land beneath.

"It just buckets down," said Karen.

And each raindrop hit the ground so hard it splashed up again to waist height.

"It makes you wet both ends at once," said Jock.

All the world was waterlogged and all the world was green and growing. The garden was a jigsaw puzzle which daily filled in more of its own pieces. Mungai worked furiously, between downpours, in the vegetable garden, and Mrs. Elliott labored in the flower beds, weeding, planting out, composting, mulching, willing slaves to the rainy season.

In the plots of ground allotted to them, Joshua's

wife and Mungai's daughter planted maize and beans which seemed to shoot up almost before the planters turned their backs. And in Nairobi, wherever there was a vacant lot or unclaimed patch of ground, Kikuyu women planted beans, so that the modern bustling town took on a satisfyingly rural aspect.

But indoors, life was depressing. Laundry dripped on makeshift lines, muddy shoes cluttered the doormats, and umbrellas lay in wait for the unwary. Tina looked long-suffering and Ajax sighed gustily.

Karen's discontent continued with the rain. She saw the holidays slipping away and none of her plans were carried out. The big boys shut themselves up together for hours on end, or talked of things that did not interest her; while Jock hobnobbed with Kukombe in the Faulkners' kitchen, learning to make bread, or joked with the stable hands behind the house. He would willingly have haunted the Elliotts' kitchen, too, but Karen snapped at him and he withdrew.

For a while it seemed to Karen as if everything that made life worth living had vanished—she had lost in quick succession her dream, the puppies and Richard.

Yet although the leopard was safely out of the way, things still did not seem back to normal. Since the puppies had left, Tina often shared her bedroom, and sometimes Karen would wake, deep in the night, and hear Tina growl or see her stand with her front feet on the window seat, staring out into the darkness. What prowled around the house in the small hours? Ajax dashed off as usual when released in the morning. "Is he full of reckless courage, or just dumb?" wondered Karen. But surely Tina stayed closer to home. She had a feeling of tension, as if she were waiting for something to happen. "But what could happen now the leopard has gone?" she asked herself.

She didn't try to discuss this feeling with her mother. It would, she felt, be put down to her age or the state of her digestion. And Richard, her usual confidant, was out of reach.

Instead, for comfort she turned, as always, to animals. Two delightful newcomers were a pair of striped mice she discovered creeping out from under the hedge morning and evening. They came to steal the grains of rice scattered on the path by the dogs as they wolfed their dinners outside, weather permitting. Karen longed to catch one, but they were far too wary.

The sinister tortoise was not one of her successes. She never quite overcame her dislike of the snaky head; and, in any case, it had to be kept out of Joshua's sight. So one day she dashed out and returned it to the bush. She watched it battling with the undergrowth until it sank out of sight among a jungle of new-grown grass.

She groomed the dogs and she exercised her hunting spider daily, on the veranda when the weather allowed, but sometimes in the sitting room. Here, one day, she absent-mindedly left him, when she was called to help with Jenny.

Mrs. Elliott came in half an hour later to finish

some mending. She had just plunked herself down, with her sewing basket on her knee, when the spider raced across her foot.

"Eeeeeow!" screamed Mrs. Elliott. She scrambled to her feet, sending the basket of oddments flying.

Joshua came running from the dining room, and Karen from the bedroom. Joshua arrived first.

"Joshua, take it away!" Mrs. Elliott hugged herself with fright. Spiders were her weak point.

Joshua grabbed the spider with one broad brown hand. He straightened up and met Mrs. Elliott's eyes.

"You not like?" he asked.

"Joshua," said Mrs. Elliott with deep feeling. "To my tribe, spiders bring the worst kind of bad luck."

Joshua nodded his head in complete understanding. He carried the spider back to Karen, who stood in the doorway, trying not to giggle. Meekly she put the spider away and returned to help hunt for spools.

It was about this time that the noises in the roof began. Pitter-patter, pitter-patter, went small invisible feet, skittering over the ceiling. Karen lay in bed, night after night, staring into the darkness and hearing *thump-scurry-scuffle, thump-scurry-scuffle* as something busied itself over her head. Soon the unknown creatures became bolder. The pattering could be heard in the early evening, not only over the bedrooms but over the bathroom and kitchen as well.

And then Mrs. Elliott noticed something else. She called to Karen.

"Such an odd thing, dear. There are hundreds of dead bees in a heap outside the kitchen."

"They'll just be the ones the ants killed, won't they?" said Karen, not really thinking.

"After all this rain? And with all the *dudus* about to eat them? You know how everything gets tidied up in Africa. Though they are right underneath the entrance to the nest."

Karen frowned, staring down at the pathetic mound of corpses. "It looks just as if something has pushed them out of the nest," she said slowly. "What on earth could have done that? I wonder if the nest has a new tenant?"

"Whatever it is, it must be a good housekeeper," said Mrs. Elliott, smiling. Her smile faded later that morning when she thought to question Joshua. He replied with one word, and a shrug of expressive shoulders.

"Panya," said Joshua. "They live in the roof," he added.

"Rats? Oh no," said Mrs. Elliott. That rats were plentiful, she was well aware; the dogs often hunted them in the long grass. They were field rats, big, strong and destructive, but without the sewer associations which cling to town rats. Even so, Mrs. Elliott could not relish the idea of sharing her house with them.

"What are they after up there?" she asked in a cross voice. "Rats can't live on tiny crumbs, like dormice."

"It is the honey," said Joshua. "The honey in the roof."

Mrs. Elliott stared at him. "You mean, first we had the bees to put up with? Then they brought the ants down on us? And now we are to be pestered with rats, all because of those same wretched bees?"

"Ndio, Memsahib," said Joshua, understanding one word in five, but getting the gist.

"Well!" said Mrs. Elliott indignantly. She went away to tell Karen. Karen had hoped for something more exciting, a wild cat with kittens, or a family of mongoose. However, after that, when she lay in bed listening to the busy little feet scampering to and fro, she clothed the sounds with coats of fur, long naked tails and twitching whiskers. "Rats in the roof," she whispered to herself. "Some people have bats in their belfries; we have rats in our roof!"

By the beginning of the third, and last, week of the Easter holidays, which was also the last week in April, the rain had slackened, though the days were cool and overcast. Released from house arrest, and able to give free rein to her under-exercised legs, Karen regained her normal good temper and accepted Jock as a confederate, second best but better than nothing.

"But I still feel disgruntled," she said to him on Tuesday, when Richard and Angus had gone off somewhere without them once again. (And the blind for bird-watching was still unmade.)

"Like a warthog with tonsilitis?" asked Jock helpfully. Karen had to laugh.

"That's it exactly," she said.

They were wandering aimlessly around the garden and pulled up next to Mrs. Elliott, who was leaning over the vegetable garden fence, talking to Mungai. They leaned also.

"Look at the lettuces!" she said to them. "Poor Mungai. He works so hard and everything was doing so well. But a bushbuck must have been in here last night. Half the young lettuces gone! And the tomato plants trampled. We'll have to build a better fence."

Karen opened the gate and went to examine the small pointed hoofmarks stamped into the earth. She trailed them across the beds of flourishing greenery to one corner of the garden, where the fence was leaning outwards. "I think he jumped in here," she called over her shoulder.

"What?" yelled Jock from the other side of the garden.

"He must have . . ." Karen stopped in mid-sentence. She had caught sight of something. In front of her, crossing the far corner of the plot, were one or two different imprints, round, large and blunt. Paw marks. Karen's heart stopped dead, rewound itself, and ticked on. She dropped on her knees and peered at the prints. "Oh," she said, under her breath. "Are you back? Or did you never leave?"

Jock came bounding over the beds to join her. His feet landed in soft deep earth and he skidded, heels braking furiously, straight across the prints, erasing them completely and showering Karen with earth.

"Oh Jock!" said Karen, spitting earth.

"Oh crumbs, sorry," said Jock. "If I had a tail I'd tuck it between my legs." He reached out a hand to help her to her feet just as Karen began to stand up. He knocked her over.

Karen sat among the cabbages and looked at him. She began to laugh. It was just no good being angry with Jock.

"Anyway," said Jock, when Karen had found her feet, "Mungai wants to set some snares. Your Mum is talking him out of it. He says Sabuni does it all the time." Sabuni worked for Mrs. Liversedge.

"Well, Daddy won't have it. And Mr. Faulkner just about raises the roof," said Karen. "Poor old Ajax was nearly strangled in a snare last year. It's a wicked way to die."

"Urrrrrrk!" said Jock, rolling his eyes, sticking out his tongue, and letting his neck hang awry. He pretended to gasp for breath and Karen pushed him into the cabbage patch, and the talk ended in a chase.

The last days slipped by. Jock and Karen played with Jenny and exercised the dogs. They went to town with Mrs. Elliott. They bird-watched and explored Karen's "jungle." Sometimes it rained, sometimes it didn't. The grass went on growing, and the rats rustled in the roof.

For the last Saturday an expedition was planned. It had been too wet for riding for some time. On Saturday, it was hoped, they would all ride out toward the hills.

"Tomorrow," said Karen, as she prepared for bed on Friday evening. "Tomorrow's the last real day of the holidays. Sunday doesn't count. Tomorrow I'll go riding with Richard. If it doesn't rain.

"Tomorrow we'll have fun."

16

Wild Pigs

The leopardess had made a kill, a good kill. Bush pig was a delicacy that came her way less often than baboon or dik-dik. She was hungry, keenly hungry, for she had the cubs to feed, and she crouched over the still-warm body, eyes closing a little with pleasure as she began at once to eat. The pig was small, half grown, a youngster, but would provide her with food for more than one meal.

The forest around her was still. She had crouched in a tree, shoulder blades hunched higher than head, watching and waiting until the piglet had rootled its way beneath her, its eyes and nose muffled in rotting leaves, its ears baffled by noise of its own making. Nearby, out of sight, other snorts and other snuffles betrayed the presence of other pigs. Silently she had leaped, with metal-rigid forelegs and widespread claws, and the kill had been swift. The piglet had squealed before it died, its killer still unseen, and as the squeal faded from the air, so had the breath died in its body. At the same time all other sounds had ceased, the snorting of the pigs, the homely night sounds of nightjar, owl, bushbaby, cricket, frog. Now all that could be heard was tearing teeth, crunching bone, rough tongue on flesh.

All at once there were fresh sounds—of twigs brushed aside, leaves crushed. The sound of low angry grunting. Something was forcing its way through the undergrowth toward her.

The leopardess raised her head and listened. The sounds came closer and she shook her head impatiently, droplets of blood scattering from her whiskers. Then she snarled into the waiting night, a warning snarl, her black lips curling back from her white teeth. Keep off, said the snarl. I have killed, I am eating. This food is mine. Keep off.

But the grunting grew louder. And now, belatedly, the leopardess began to drag the carcass toward the nearest tree. But she did not reach it.

Into the glade burst two adult bush pigs, their white faces and long snouts ghostly in the moonlight. Their rush carried them past the leopardess, who tensed behind the body of her prey, flattened her ears, and snarled again. Their musty scent had reached her and her snarl carried arrogance, not fear. She had made her kill and wanted only to be left alone to eat. Pig smell meant food, not danger.

The wild pigs had seen her. They stood for a moment, shoulder to shoulder, flat snouts lowered, little eyes glowing redly. They came toward her, slowly at first, grunting as if in self-encouragement. Then, increasing speed, they charged the startled leopardess, slashing at her with savage tusks, so that she reared back on her haunches behind the sheltering carcass and lashed out in self-defense. The pigs wheeled, avoiding the piglet's body, and returned to the attack, their bulky bodies teetering on small trotters.

The unexpected assault had taken the leopardess off guard. But only for a moment. Growling with rage she sprang at the leading pig, digging her claws into its shoulders and seeking to sink her teeth into its throat; but before her teeth went home she was jolted from the body as the second pig crashed full into her side and its tusks savaged her flank. She twisted as she fell and clawed with all four feet at the nearest belly, ripping through the coarse chestnut hair and tough hide, before the pig tore loose. Then the second pig was on her, trampling with cloven hooves, rooting at her body with the short sharp tusks, squealing with rage, while she coughed and snarled and fought ferociously.

The pigs fell back, and she regained her feet with one lithe spring and crouched, waiting. They were now between her and her prey, the food she needed, and this honed her rage, whetted her savagery.

If they had stayed together she could have dealt with them, but they separated and came at her from both sides at once, and the onetime-peaceful glade resounded to the sounds of cracking branches, thudding bodies, harsh panting and screams of pain. Time and again the leopardess fought her way to the body of her victim and time and again the pigs drove her back, their anger seemingly increasing as they caught the scent of the partly eaten body.

They circled the body as if on guard, grunting ceaselessly, blood tricking from innumerable claw and teeth punctures, froth, blood and mud staining their snouts. One pig lagged behind the other, slowing, weakening now from the deep wounds in its belly, but still strong with the strength of obstinacy. The leopardess circled the pigs, snaking through the lank grass and dank thickets, her silky spotted fur matted with blood. She favored one paw, badly torn by a razor-sharp hoof, and paused in her stalking to lick the wound.

Then, knowing she was tiring, making one last attempt, she gathered her full strength and charged between the pigs, regaining her position by the carcass. This she seized by the hindquarters, crouching for the spring that would take her, and her prey, high into a tree, safe, out of reach. But she could not fight and hoist at the same time; their tusks raked her haunches and destroyed her balance. She dropped the piglet and could not regain her hold.

Then they thrust her back, their bodies a living barrier between her and her kill, and she spat at them with snarling hate and turned and leaped from the glade, and they shuffled in her wake, grunting as they came, searching the thickets, until they were sure she was gone.

She had eaten a little but needed more. She needed to rest yet needed to return to her cubs. She was filled with conflicting pressures and her instincts, perhaps, were dulled a little, were less than trigger fine. She followed a path she had taken many times before. She knew it well. A sudden rainstorm lashed down at her as she emerged from a tangle of bush and sisal, once cultivated land now overgrown. She crossed a road, running river-wet with rain, leaped a ditch, and slunk along a dripping kei apple hedge seeking a familiar gap.

The gap smelled of dog and—something else?

Too late she felt a narrow biting wire pull tight around her neck. Panick-stricken, she sprang forward and was wrenched roughly back as the noose contracted; her snarl cracked in her throat. The wire cut deeply through fur and flesh, drawn tighter, tighter, tighter still as she struggled frantically, clawing at her neck, tearing her own skin, flailing with legs and body among the keen thorns of the kei apple.

Silently she fought for breath, sought for some defense against this terrible unseen enemy. For the second time that night she battled for her life.

Finally, exhausted, she slumped among the strips of sodden bark, the drift of tawny eucalyptus leaves, the tufts of wiry grass. Her markings blended with her surroundings.

The rain beat mercilessly down.

17

Death of a Dream

Saturday dawned bright and fair. Karen woke shortly after six-thirty, roused by the endless practicing of the birds. She lay in bed and watched the treetops turn to gold as the sun gained strength. Her heart leaped at the sight of the sunshine, her toes twitched, and it was quite impossible to stay in bed one moment longer. She knelt on her window seat and watched a flock of fire finches peck their way along the path. It had rained during the night; the path was dark with damp and the gutters wept slow tears. But now there was not a cloud in sight.

"It AINTA gonna RAIN, no MORE, no MORE," sang Karen, forgetful of sleepy parents. It would, of course, but at the moment, it didn't seem to matter. It was wonderful to see the sun again.

"It's a day for something exciting to happen—an adventurous sort of a day," she thought, jiggling on one leg as she pulled on her jeans. She remembered that other day, the first day of the rains, when the magic in the air had enticed her out and she had seen the leopard.

Now it was the sun that beckoned.

As she brushed her hair back from her face, ready to twist it high on her head in its accustomed ponytail, she saw, from her window Mungai come up through the trees and move off behind the hedge. He carried a panga and was collecting wood to dry in the sun and store for kindling. Karen began to call out to him, forgetting that she held an elastic band between her teeth. She spluttered, dropped the band, and groped for it on her knees, one-handed, still holding her hair with the other hand. When she stood up Mungai was out of sight.

"*Jambo!*" A cheerful greeting rang out from the plot next door. Sabuni also was out early, perhaps on the same errand.

"Eh, *Jambo! Habari?*" That was Mungai's deep voice replying.

Karen finished her hair and bent down to slip on her sandals. Then she turned to look for a sweater.

It was at that moment that the most appalling din broke out, a cacophony of harsh snarls and screams and shouts.

Karen dashed back to the window. The noise came from the direction of the road, but nothing was visible behind the high green hedge. She made for the door. The noise was so all-pervading that she ran through the house without bothering to be quiet; no one would sleep through that uproar.

Outside the air tasted cold and sweet and tangy. Karen ran as if the devil were at her heels round the inner hedge and on through the long grass toward the road. She could see Sabuni leaping up and down. He was yelling at the top of his voice. Mungai, panga raised, half crouched behind a stump of tree.

And in the ragged thorny hedge that edged her land something gold and black and frantic clawed and struggled and screeched.

It was the leopard.

Karen could not remember later her arrival on the scene. Suddenly she was there, and Mungai had her fast by the arm and held her back at a safe distance from the raging, maddened animal. She found herself whispering, over and over again: "Help her, help her, help her . . ." though she knew Mungai could not understand her, even if he heard her. And the source of the trouble was plain. The leopard was caught in a wire snare concealed in the hedge. There was blood around its mouth and its eyes were wild with pain and fright.

Mungai was trying to thrust her back towards the house.

"Kwenda, Missy, kwenda upesi!" he shouted at her.

Sabuni still leaped and yelled.

More Africans had joined them, some, on their way to work, peering curiously from the road,

143

others running down from neighborhood houses to see what was happening.

Karen's face streamed with tears. She struggled with Mungai, resisting his efforts to send her home, not knowing why she did so. Suddenly an idea broke through. Mr. Faulkner would know what to do; it was he who had trapped the lions the previous year. He could save her leopard.

Pulling away from Mungai she fled along the inside of the hedge, panting and stumbling. Dimly she caught sight of her parents, hastily dressed, running across the grass. They called to her but she paid no attention, only saved her breath for running. Never had it taken so long to cover the familiar distance between the houses.

The Faulkners and their guests were at breakfast at the back of the house, out of earshot of the pandemonium by the road. Karen burst in on them unannounced. Her face was scarlet and streaked with dirt and tears; her hair, tugged from its neat topknot by clutching branches, straggled round her cheeks and down her neck. She was so distraught and breathless that she could only gasp, while they stared at her in dumb consternation. Then she recovered her voice, and, clinging to Mr. Faulkner's sleeve, poured out her story, pulling at him to bring him to his feet and interrupting herself to tell him to hurry, hurry, *hurry!*

Mr. Faulkner looked grim. Without a word he disengaged himself from Karen's frantic hand and left the room, while the others clustered round her, trying to make her sit down and rest. But Karen stayed on her feet, twisting her hands painfully together and trembling so hard that her teeth chattered.

"Oh, why doesn't he hurry, why doesn't he hurry?" she whispered.

Mr. Faulkner shouted to them from the veranda and at once Karen shot out of the door and led the race through the garden. Mr. Faulkner loped along close behind her and Richard stayed by her side, urging her to slow down. She tripped and almost fell, and he caught her arm, but she pulled away and ran on.

A small crowd of wide-eyed spectators huddled by the road, poised as if ready to run. The noise had lessened; there was only the subdued buzz of conversation punctuated by occasional dry coughs and rasping breaths from the exhausted leopard.

Karen ran until she reached Mungai, who, still armed with his panga, stood with the Elliotts a little way back from the scene. A new figure now caught her eye. Mrs. Liversedge, complete with leather gaiters and broad-brimmed hat, self-possessed and in command, stood to one side of the panting, straining leopard.

In her hands she held a rifle.

Karen stopped short and stared.

"Oh no!" she gasped. "No, Mrs. Liversedge. You can't shoot this one, not this one. Mr. Faulkner— Mr. Faulkner, you can get her out, can't you?" Her voice rose hysterically as she realized, for the first time, that Mr. Faulkner also carried a rifle.

"Karen. Be quiet." Mr. Faulkner spoke sharply

and clearly. It was a voice to obey. Karen gulped and subsided, her face whitewash-white beneath the tear stains. Her mother came quickly to her side.

"Come home, dear. Karen, come home," she begged.

But Karen stood as stiff and pale and immovable as if she had been turned to a pillar of salt.

Mrs. Liversedge acknowledged Mr. Faulkner's presence with a curt nod.

"Nasty!" she said abruptly. "Sabuni was collecting wood. Leopard dashed nearly got him. Badly hurt. Has to be shot. No other way."

Mr. Faulkner grunted agreement. "Get those people out of harm's way," he said to Richard, who was off in a flash to the road, to clear the spectators well out of the line of fire.

There was a faint click as Mr. Faulkner removed the safety catch. A hush fell over the scene. Even the leopard paused in its struggles, its teeth bared in a grimace, its tormented eyes glaring straight at the man. Mr. Faulkner moved forward a little, quietly. The rifle came smoothly up to his shoulder.

Karen shut her eyes.

There was a sudden crash which seemed to grow in her head and explode in a million aching stars behind her lids. A second crash. And then there was nothing.

Slowly Karen opened her eyes.

The leopard slumped amid the thorns. Her mother's arms held her; Richard was saying something

urgently to her. And Jock, his chubby face full of distress, tugged at her sleeve.

Karen tore herself loose from her mother's grasp. She ran away from them all, her parents, her friends, her neighbors, the onlookers, and stumbled back through the garden, under the trees and on past the rondavels where Joshua's plump wife stood and stared, her baby on her hip. On she went, through the wilderness of bush, until, exhausted and bent from the stitch in her side, she reached the murram pit and fell on the damp grass to cry and mourn and try to remember the leopard, her leopard, so beautiful, confident and free, as she had first seen it in the tree beyond the pool.

Ajax found her there. The dogs had been released when the Elliotts returned to the house and, far though she was from home, he soon discovered her. He did not intrude on her but lay close by her side, his eyes on her prostrate form, his nose near her hand. After a while Karen grew conscious of his comforting presence. She reached out and stroked his head and neck. Soon she sat up, rubbing her smarting eyes, pushing back her tangled hair from her hot and throbbing forehead.

"Ajax. Dear Ajax," she murmured. He pushed against her, eagerly now, sure of his welcome and wriggling with pleasure, and she buried her face in his mane and hugged him to her.

Later she began to think more calmly. Her tears ceased. She blew her nose and mopped her eyes. Her clothes were damp from the grass but the sun was shining warmly now. She looked at the sun and guessed that the morning was far advanced. She stretched, and realized that she was both hungry and thirsty.

Karen rose stiffly to her feet. She felt tired but calm and not unhappy. She snapped her fingers and Ajax came to her side, and together they walked back toward the house.

18

Inquest

Joshua was the first person Karen saw on her return to the house. He opened the kitchen door for her and she went in, leaving Ajax to attend to his own affairs.

"You want breakfast?" Joshua asked, his brown eyes fixed anxiously on her, his face poised to split into a smile at the first sign that it would be welcome.

"Oh yes, please!" said Karen. Her stomach was nudging her spine. She noticed that all the breakfast things had been cleared away and that Joshua was in the middle of peeling potatoes. "Can you manage an egg?" she asked. "Bread will do—don't bother about toast."

Joshua nodded, and Karen slipped quietly down the passage to wash her face and tidy her hair before she met anyone else. She caught a hum of conversation from the sitting room; several people must be there, she thought.

When she returned to the kitchen a thick slice of ham was sizzling in the frying pan, and Joshua was just breaking an egg into the hot fat. Already there was a tantalizing aroma of toast, and a glass of creamy milk stood ready on the top of the refrigerator.

"Oh Joshua. You angel!" said Karen.

Her mouth watered. She was feeling better by the minute. When the food was ready, she perched on the kitchen stool and ate off the counter. She learned from Joshua that both Mr. Faulkner and Mrs. Liversedge were in the sitting room with her parents, as well as the boys.

She was just thanking Joshua for taking such trouble with her belated breakfast when Jock appeared in the doorway, his nose quivering as he tracked down the alluring odors of ham and toast.

"Hallo, Karen, you pig," he said briskly. "I bet you've finished everything worth eating!"

Karen looked at him shyly, expecting questions, but Jock found half a slice of buttered toast still sitting on her plate and skillfully whisked it away. He seemed intent on munching, and Karen stood up and brushed the crumbs from her lap. She squared her shoulders, breathed deeply, and walked toward the sitting room.

Mr. Faulkner stood with his back to the empty fireplace. Karen walked straight up to him, swallowed, and said quickly, "I'm very sorry I was so silly, Mr. Faulkner. I shouldn't have made such a fuss."

Mr. Faulkner looked gravely down at her. Then he smiled. "I'm sorry too, Karen, for what I had to do. I think you know that. If I'd thought there was any way to save the leopard, I'd have tried. But in a place like that, with people crowding round, and the animal badly injured, I just couldn't take a chance. If the leopard had torn loose from the snare she might well have killed anybody who got in her way.

"Oh yes, sometimes—if one has the proper drugs and instruments on hand—it is possible to put a wounded animal to sleep while it is tended and caged, but I wasn't prepared for that. It was better for the leopard the way it was.

"If we could only teach people not to set snares a lot of misery would be spared. They rarely kill outright; they maim and torture the victim who slowly suffocates or dies from exhaustion and loss of blood after struggling for hours. Some trapped animals die from starvation, after days of misery." He turned to Mrs. Liversedge. "I think the culprit this time is Sabuni, you know. I heard him talking to his friends. He wasn't after firewood this morning; he was making the rounds of his snares when the leopard clawed at him. I hope the fright he got will put him off trapping for a while."

Conversation became general again. Karen sat down on a footstool and let the noise flow over her head. Then she was conscious of Mr. Faulkner questioning her.

"Remember, Karen, when we saw the leopard on the driveway? You seemed to think it was a female. But that was a male. This morning again you seemed sure it was a female. This time it was. But what made you so sure? Just a guess?"

"I saw her once before," said Karen in a small voice; but, just at that moment, there came a lull in the conversation and her voice carried clearly.

"Saw her before? When? Where?"

"The first day of the rains—that morning I went out tracking." Karen glanced around the suddenly silent room and found that everyone was staring at her. She turned pink. "I followed some footprints from outside my bedroom right down past the murram pit. Oh, it was smashing! It was early in the morning; there was no one in the world but me! I nearly lost her once but just by chance I went toward your woodland—the monkeys were fussing." Karen took a timid peep at Mrs. Liversedge sitting massive and silent on the sofa. "And when I turned a corner there she was, sitting in a tree washing her face and purring at me. She was the most beautiful thing I had ever seen!" Karen ended in a rush. She had just caught sight of her mother's face.

"Karen Elliott! You followed a leopard right through the bush by yourself at daybreak!"

"I didn't know I was following a leopard," Karen said hastily. But honesty compelled her to add: "But I did hope it was. I mean, I'd never seen any footprints like that before, and I knew there weren't many creatures that could make them. But it was

153

sort of a game—you know? I never really thought I'd catch up with her."

"Karen!"

"Well, Mum, if she hadn't trodden on your flower bed I'd never have known and I'd probably still have gone down there—it was that sort of morning. Up and doing-ish. Mr. Faulkner says there are lots of leopards about, really. Lurking in odd places. We just don't see them. But we can't stay indoors all the time because of that." Karen's tone was soothing and reasonable, but her mother still looked at her with doubt in her eyes.

"But that doesn't explain how you knew it was a leopardess," persisted Richard.

"Oh, I just knew. Like when you look at Tina and Ajax? You'd never take Tina for a male. The male leopard was much bigger and its face was tougher, less feline. I was puzzled about him, because it didn't seem likely there would be two, when I'd never even seen one before. I thought maybe his swollen face made the difference. But when I saw her this morning, I knew at once. That first time, she was being feminine and thinking about her looks, and grooming herself after the rain. Girl stuff. We looked at each other and she was friendly."

"And after that she was your leopard?" It was Mr. Faulkner who spoke.

"Yes."

"Well, I think you're bonkers, man! A crazy cat, wow, two crazy cats!" said Jock, who was standing in the doorway, all ears. "It might have jumped you."

"Oh no," said Karen. "I stayed very still and then just backed away politely."

"And the leopardess minded her manners too?"

"Yes."

Jock grinned, and Karen's father grunted.

"Well, you know now, Karen, after our narrow escape in the park, if you didn't know before, just how dangerous a leopard can be. Bear it in mind."

As Mr. Faulkner stopped speaking, Mrs. Liversedge rose, and Dogo appeared from under the sofa like a rabbit out of a top hat.

"Well, young lady, if you were mine you'd get a good spanking." She frowned down at Karen, who made herself as small as possible on her stool, while Dogo sat at his mistress's side with a disapproving air. Then a sudden twinkle brightened Mrs. Liversedge's faded blue eyes. "I must confess I would have followed the footprints myself," she said unexpectedly. She turned to Mrs. Elliott. "She's a good gel. And the type they need for a new independent Kenya. My generation of Europeans came here and killed—oh, we thought we had reason. We killed for food, we protected ourselves and our stock. We were pioneers. I was fifteen when I shot my first lion.

"But we killed unreasonably, too. Called it a 'sport.' Boasted about it. Decorated our houses with skulls and horns and skins. Now the poachers are carrying on the bad work for money, not amusement. It's up to the younger generation to do something to repair the damage we did. Though even the old 'uns can help. We owe it to Africa. Bah, I'm

a sentimental old fool, and I'm making a speech!"
She strode toward the door. "I shall now go and
make Sabuni show me all his other snares. Hah!"

Mr. Faulkner also headed for the door. "Time I
did some work," he said. "A friend of mine wants
me to look after his young zebra for a few weeks
while he goes to Uganda, gorilla spotting," he
added. "And he says it's a pest, into everything.
So we're going to start on a good strong enclosure
today. Oh and Karen, there's one thing more I
meant to tell you. That leopardess of yours has
cubs tucked away somewhere—pity we don't know
where. Can't be more than a few weeks old. She
was in full milk."

Karen had pricked up her ears at the mention of
the zebra, but the end of Mr. Faulkner's speech
took her breath away. Then, as the boys followed
him out on to the veranda, where Mrs. Liversedge
lingered, admiring the roses, she found her tongue.

"Richard, did you hear what your father said?
Did you know? About the cubs? We can't just leave
them, they'll starve! We'll have to hunt for them."

"Well, where? They could be anywhere, Karen.
Be reasonable. Anyway, the best bet is back in the
game park. Leopards come and go all the time.
They know they aren't molested there. With any
luck a game ranger will come across the cubs. I
know you'd like to try to find 'em, Karen, but that's
a game. It's not real. Today's the first fine morning
in ages and the horses need exercise. And this afternoon we're helping Dad with the zebra enclosure."

He looked at her, and the fine-drawn look of her

face reminded him of her misery that morning. "Don't fret about the cubs, Karen. It's not your fault," he said gently. "Come riding with us and cheer yourself up. We won't get to the hills now, but it'll be fun."

This was yesterday's dream come true. But Karen shook her head. "No thank you, not today," she said. Then, seemingly forgetting the subject of leopards, she questioned Richard eagerly about the zebra.

"Of course you can come and see it," said Richard impatiently. "You half live at our house anyway." Angus punched him in the ribs to attract his attention, and he turned, punching back, and they moved away. "See you," he said. Jock followed them.

Karen sat on the veranda steps and watched the boys ambling down the path, looking from behind, she thought, like two giraffes escorting a warthog. She propped her chin in her hands and frowned hard at nothing. Where would a leopard make its lair? An idea sparked. The old quarry? That wasn't far, just at the end of Quarry Lane. But almost at once she remembered that part of the quarry was still worked. There were men and trucks, noise and bustle. No self-respecting leopard would make its home in such a place.

A cold nose snuffled her ankle and she found Dogo by her side. Mrs. Liversedge loomed over her.

"Years ago," she barked, "leopards lived on the escarpment. Overlooking the game park. Good place, that. Quiet. That's where I'd live, if I were a leopard." She whistled to Dogo and marched off without saying good-by.

"Cubs," thought Karen. "My leopardess had cubs. The escarpment. I know where that is. Cubs. . . ."

19

Cubs Alone

The cubs were alone.

The leopardess had been gone for more than twelve hours, and they were cold and hungry. Never before had she left them as long as this. They huddled together in the rear of the cave where the mother smell was strongest, two dappled balls of fur seeking warmth from the contact of their own tiny bodies but moving restlessly, each striving for the cosiest spot beneath the other, yet shrinking away from the cold touch of the stone floor on either side of them.

Their parched mouths sucked emptily. Lips smacked at nothing, thirsting pink tongues seeking milk found fur. They mumbled urgently at each other's necks, ears, paws. Spat hair. Mewed.

They slept and woke. Outside the cave the sun

was high in the sky, a glowing, life-giving ball. Lizards lay inert on rocks soaking up the golden heat of noon. The damp earth steamed. Birdsong faded as songsters slept. In the game park zebra and wildebeest sought shade, stood heads to haunches beneath the thorny branches, only their tails alive as they swished away the droning biting flies. The pride of lions panted in their resting place.

But the cubs were cold. Splinters of light made patterns on the baked-earth floor at the entrance to the cave, dazzling their newly opened, milk-blue eyes. They stayed at the rear, shunning the light, yet turning toward it, knowing that this was the way their mother would return.

Overhead a herd of fleecy clouds strayed westward. A shape glided, wings motionless, lifting and turning, buoyed up by the ascending warmth. Keen eyes searched the escarpment, spied a basking lizard. The kite swooped, plummeted down, screamed triumphantly as it snatched its prey from the rock. Its shadow cut across the dusty sunbeams dancing at the cave entrance.

One cub, the male, startled by the sound, puzzled by the sudden movement, rolled away from his sister's comforting body and staggered weakly toward the spot where briefly the shadow splashed. Abandoned, the second cub mewed angrily, protestingly, then followed on bent wobbling legs, hollow belly brushing stone, behind her brother.

At the edge of the sunlight the male cub stopped. He dabbed with one small paw at the shreds of light, overbalanced, and collapsed, eyes tight shut in protest at the strangeness. But the warmth of the sunlit floor pleased him, and he stayed where he had fallen. His sister tucked herself against him, snuggled close, whimpered softly.

They slept again.

20

The Search

Karen roused herself. Her thoughts had been miles away, visiting the orphaned cubs, wherever they might be.

She went indoors to tidy her bedroom, dust her books, and try to put in order the thoughts tumbling round inside her head. She peered in her mirror. Her eyelids were pink and puffy but otherwise she looked much as usual. But she felt a good deal older than when she had bounced out of bed that morning, full of the joy of living.

She had now accepted the death of her dream leopard but she could not put out of her mind the picture of the leopard cubs, forlorn, abandoned, starving, somewhere in a rocky crevice or cave where soon they would be found by jackals. It did not make sense to her that a leopard hunting regularly outside the game park should yet rear her family within the park. The nearest gorge or valley in the park which came to mind was Kingfisher Gorge, and that was ten miles away. A healthy leopard should have had no trouble finding food close at hand. But if the cubs were somewhere outside the park. . . .

Karen sat down on the end of her bed and pondered. The escarpment. Some of the most attractive houses in Langata were built near its edge; the view was fabulous. But there were still long stretches untouched, as wild as they had ever been. It was not far away. Beyond her own garden there lay the golf course, and then Bogani Road, and then more houses and plots, some developed, some overgrown with wattle and thorn. On again, and there it was. Or was it?

Karen ran from the room, out of the house, and down the garden path. The glove compartment of her father's car was choked with maps—maps torn, maps dog-eared, maps sticky with barley sugar where Jenny had fingered them. She shuffled her way through them till she found a local ordnance map. Back in her room she spread the map over her bed. Carefully she checked her direction and estimated the distance. Perhaps two miles, perhaps a little more. She could easily walk it.

By the time her mother called her to a late lunch she had formed a plan. The sun was still shining; it was the first really fine day for some considerable time. It was natural that she should want to be out. Mrs. Elliott herself was hoping for a delicious afternoon with the power mower, her favorite toy. Karen asked permission to go exploring, promising to take Ajax with her, promising to be sensible.

But it was not a day when things went smoothly. Her mother gave her consent only if the boys would be going also. Karen mumbled agreement but behind her back she crossed her fingers. She longed for company but would not approach Richard again. She would manage on her own.

She was not yet free to start, however. First she was pressed into minding Jenny while Mrs. Elliott drove to the shops—an errand left over from the morning. Her mother was delayed and at two o'clock Karen put Jenny down in her cot for her afternoon nap and waited impatiently for the sound of the car. She packed a knapsack with her binoculars, water flask, chocolate and an old pair of leather gloves. She poked the gloves in at the last minute, it having occurred to her that if she did find a family of leopard cubs they might be difficult to handle. She changed her sandals for strong shoes, and carried her windbreaker.

The time dragged by. At last her mother returned. Then it was necessary to hunt for Ajax. She was, in fact, pinning her hopes on him. If he really had an instinct for tracking her venture might succeed.

There was still one last errand to do before she set out. Reluctantly she returned to the stretch of hedge where the leopard had met its death. There, among the thorns, she found a tuft of dull golden fur, leopard fur.

Mungai, spotless in his Salvation Army uniform,

sailed down the road on his bicycle, and she waved to him. Then she captured Ajax and clipped his leash, half chain, half leather, to his collar. She was ready, but she hesitated, looking wistfully toward the neighboring garden. She could hear occasional shouts and the sound of hammering. The boys were hard at work on their zebra enclosure.

Karen sighed. Then she patted Ajax and held the tuft of fur to his nose. "Find, Ajax. Find the leopard. Good boy, you can do it."

She led him over the area of crushed and trampled grass, wincing away from blood stains, and aimed him gardenwards.

"Find, Ajax, find. Good dog."

Ajax whined and sniffed unhappily. He did not like the scent of leopard, nor the scent of death. He licked Karen's hand to show his goodwill, then sat down and scratched.

"Oh Ajax, come on!" said Karen in despair. She gnawed her little fingernail. At that moment she heard a whistle, loud, cheerful and off-key, and Ajax bounded toward the hedge, jerking the leash from her hand.

Jock appeared in the gap in the hedge, his battered hat slapped on the back of his head.

Karen stared at him, and a slow smile appeared on her face.

"What happened, did they throw you out?" she asked.

Jock looked hurt. "Of course not," he said. "It was just that there were only two hammers, so Angus and I took turns, and I only hit his fingers once or twice, but he makes such a bloomin' fuss about little things."

Karen grinned. "Too bad," she said. "Want to come with me? I'm going to look for the leopard cubs."

Jock whistled again, long and low this time. "Where?"

"The escarpment. It's a bit of a walk. Think you're strong enough?"

"How long a walk?"

"Oh, as long as a piece of string—as my Granny used to say. Ajax is going to track the cubs for me."

"Oh yeah?" said Jock, but he looked interested.

"If you want to come, come now," said Karen firmly. "No going back home for supplies, or emergency rations, or whatever you call it."

"I've got some chewing gum," said Jock. He chewed furiously to prove it.

"Then let's go," said Karen. But first they had to recapture Ajax, who was digging for mole rats.

"Now he's got his nose all earthy," said Karen in disgust.

"But you don't need him now, muffin," said Jock. "You know where you're going. So let's go the quickest route, and when we get to the escarpment, *then* we can get Ajax on the job. Maybe. Anyway, if the leopard was going home, not coming from home, there won't be a trail."

Karen looked at him, her jaw dropping. "Jeepers," she said. "You're right. And I thought Angus was the brain. What a good job you turned up."

Jock looked complacent. "Oh, I'm not just a

pretty face, you know." Karen twisted her own face into a hideous grimace. Then, feeling pleased with themselves, they set off down the plot, Ajax leading the way proudly as though it was his idea.

It didn't take long to reach the golf course, and they climbed through the fence. As it was a Saturday afternoon, and a fine day, they ran the gauntlet of irritated golfers, and Ajax objected strongly to the rude shouts of "fore" which greeted them regularly. As quickly as they could they left the course and scrambled through another fence onto the roadway.

Here they paused as the Vicar shot down the road in his battle-scarred Mini-Minor, the strap of his bird-watching binoculars plainly visible on his shoulders.

There were no houses in sight on that stretch of the road. They crossed over and entered a plantation of young gums where Ajax at once showed signs of excitement. When he sniffed around and whined, Karen could not resist presenting him once more with the scrap of leopard fur. His head went down and he made off at a good pace, towing Karen along behind him like a large tug with a small ocean liner. Jock, chewing and panting, trotted in the rear.

Soon he called to Karen, "Hey, you're going the wrong way!"

"What?" yelled Karen.

"The wrong way. The escarpment's over there." He pointed, and Karen, looking one way and walking another, tripped over a tree stump and barked her shin. The leash flew from her hand.

At once Ajax leapt forward, giving one almighty WHOOF, and from among the trees ahead of them fled a trim reddish-brown form. Karen shouted, Jock whistled, but Ajax raced after the duiker and vanished from sight among the trees.

"Oh bother that dog," said Karen crossly. "I hoped he was tracking the leopard. I suppose it was that buck all the time. Talk about being led by the nose!"

"Give him a chance," said Jock tolerantly. "If he did smell a leopard he'd probably run in the opposite direction anyway." Jock was glad of the rest and flopped down on the tree stump, feeling in his pocket as he did so for his packet of gum. All Jock hoped for that afternoon was a pleasant ramble and a chance of fun.

Karen accepted a piece of gum but tapped impatiently with her foot and at regular intervals called for Ajax in her most commanding voice. To her the search was deadly serious. Time was slipping by, and there had been so many delays. But Ajax took his time, and when he did return he crashed down on them in a fashion that was plainly unrepentant.

Once again they trudged on. The far side of the plantation was fenced with barbed wire, crossed and crisscrossed. After some argument they scrambled through safely with only a rip in Karen's jeans and a scratch on Jock's chubby arm where a wire pinged back at him.

Ajax left a tuft of black hair for the fence to remember him by.

Then they were in real bush, thick, wild and thorny. There were no signs of people, but the jumble of scrub and weed before them was dissected by skinny paths made by the bush dwellers. Droppings were plentiful and the path was marked by the spoor of buck and small mammals, perhaps mongoose, zorillas or jackals. To Karen the very air smelled wilder. She hushed Jock when he whistled too loudly and held Ajax on a short leash. She felt a long way from home.

It was difficult to keep track of direction. The sun was hidden from sight by the misshapen branches of the thorn trees and the little paths twisted and turned. Ajax whined excitedly and he pulled Karen this way and that, distracted by the concentration of scents. But it was he who led them, in the end, to the cliff.

"What'll you bet he's following a skunk?" asked Jock, after some time. "Even I can smell it!"

Karen frowned at him. She felt Ajax needed encouragement, not mockery. And though she was glad he was there, she was beginning to think Jock unduly frivolous. But after a while she had to admit that she too caught occasional whiffs of something unpleasant—something very dead.

"But that's just what you don't find much in Africa," she argued, mostly with herself, but out loud in case Jock was interested. "Anything dead and edible gets eaten almost before it has a chance to rot, what with hyenas and jackals, vultures, ants and dung beetles!"

"It's probably someone's rubbish pit," said Jock

prosaically. Outside the city of Nairobi there was no rubbish collection, and householders dug pits and dumped cans and refuse in them, while vegetable peelings went on a compost heap.

"What, out here?" Karen held back a thorny branch while Jock scrambled round a bush, then she pushed past a low-slung tree and found herself, at last, at the edge of the escarpment.

"Whoops!" Karen hauled at Ajax. He was standing on his hind legs in his eagerness.

They had reached the source of the smell, but Karen had no thought for anything but the scene ahead. The bushes grew nearly to the edge of the escarpment, which fell away sharply in front of them in a jumble of boulders, gravel and weathered rock. Beyond and below lay the game park and beyond again the open plains, unfenced, uncultivated, seemingly uninhabited as far as the eye could see.

Karen drew a deep breath. It was a wonderful moment, marred only by the noisome smell. "Look, Jock," she said. "Africa! Miles and miles of lovely Africa!"

"It's Africa up here too, stupid," said Jock, unimpressed.

"Oh I know. But it doesn't feel like it. Houses and roads, telephone poles and cars, people like you and me, instead of just people like Joshua and Mungai. Up here it feels like home, but down there —it's *wild*."

Jock had turned away. Now he clutched at her arm, sending her off balance. "Karen—look!"

"You look out," said Karen sharply. He had spoiled her romantic mood, and she had stumbled rather too near the edge of the cliff for comfort.

"But Karen. Don't be like that, I'm sorry, I didn't mean to grab at you—but look!"

This time Karen looked where Jock pointed. A short way to the left a black wattle tree grew taller and stronger than the surrounding scrub. And crammed in a fork near the top of the tree, staring at the children with empty eye sockets, was a horned skull. A tattered brown hide draped the branch below. Flies buzzed and settled, and the smell was nauseating.

Ajax barked furiously and strained at the lead. There was a sharp hiss, the crack and flap of heavy wings, and a vulture flew up from behind the wattle.

Karen clutched at Jock and Jock clutched at Karen. They watched the vulture until it disappeared from sight.

"Phew!"

"Cor luv a duck!"

"That was no duck," said Karen. "But I'll bet you anything you like this is a leopard's larder. Remember what Mr. Faulkner told us." She gripped Jock's arm and her eyes blazed with excitement. The rest had been guesswork but this—this was evidence.

Jock looked hastily around. "Jeepers, Karen, suppose it's the wrong leopard? I mean, it's a leopardy kind of spot all right, suppose another leopard left the buck? It might come back now!" The game was becoming too real for Jock.

"It's no good thinking that, or we might as well go home. Anyway, this larder's empty. There's nothing left worth eating. That's why she was hunting over our way." Karen looked critically at the skull. "Bushbuck, wasn't it? But what matters now is finding the cubs."

"Oh all right. If you say so. Find 'em then. But don't take too long, or it will be teatime. It feels like teatime *now*."

There were bones and horns scattered around another tree nearby, and getting Ajax away from the larder trees was quite a job. Karen reasoned that the lair would not be immediately beneath the larder. It would be too strong a pointer for scavengers. Jock reasoned that a larder would be the tree nearest to a kill. And the lair might be anywhere. But they didn't fight over it. They started to explore.

Beyond the tree to the left the bushes grew right to the edge of the cliff, so that exploring would be difficult. They turned to the right and zigzagged over the rough ground, searching for some sign, a footprint, or scratch mark on a tree, anything, to guide them.

About a dozen yards from the larder a series of flat-topped boulders led down the escarpment with almost the effect of a staircase. Karen sat down on the top step and dangled her legs. There were at least six boulders below her, leading downwards, and then there was a slope of gravel. It was most tempting.

But what could they do with Ajax?

"Tie him to a tree," said Jock, when Karen asked him. He was just as keen as she was to climb down the cliff. "We won't go too far, just look around and get the feel of it. He'll be all right for a bit."

"But he's supposed to do the tracking!"

"What—down there? Come off it, Karen."

Karen still looked doubtful. But she had no other suggestion to make; so they found a tree with a straight trunk, not too embedded in bushes (so that Ajax could not get entangled), and tied his leash firmly round the trunk. Ajax whined and panted, but he sat down obediently enough at Karen's command, and it seemed safe to leave him. After all, they wouldn't be long.

Karen went first. The rim of the cliff was deeply eroded, where rainwater had cascaded down, and it was easy to tell from the state of the cliff face that landslides were common. She tested each foothold, and each boulder, before moving on. By the time she had clambered down four of the steps the top of the cliff was barely visible. Not far below her was a steep drop. It was a strange place, wild and desolate, almost sinister. Karen shivered in the bright sunshine. She was grateful for the sight of Jock hunching himself down to join her, Jock with his comforting snub nose and rosy cheeks, his owl glasses, familiar patched khaki shorts and shabby sweater with the frayed wrists.

At first there was no sign of life. Then a hyrax darted across a grassy ledge below her, and a hawk flew up, sending its warning cry echoing along the cliff. A pied crow echoed the warning from its perch in a thorn tree.

At the bottom of the staircase Karen sat down and relaxed, while she waited for Jock. Looking back the steps appeared much steeper than they had felt coming down. Jock grunted as he dropped the last three feet and landed at her side. His thud sent a handful of gravel rattling down the slope.

"Hot work," puffed Jock. The sun, dropping now toward the distant hills, was full on them. Karen remembered her supplies. It seemed the right time to produce the water bottle, and the chocolate tasted heavenly. There wasn't nearly enough. Karen hadn't catered for two.

She was still hot and she fanned herself with Jock's old felt hat.

"What time is it?" she asked, too lazy to look for herself. Jock studied his watch which he wore with the face on the inside of his wrist, in the fashion set by his favorite television secret agent.

"Hey, it's a quarter past five! We *have* mucked about. Told you it was teatime. My inside always knows. Well, that's it then, we'd better start back now."

"No. Not yet."

"But it's high tea on Saturdays. Sausages. Lashings of 'em. And Kukombe makes gingerbread."

"But we haven't found them yet." Karen stared stubbornly around her at the secret face of the cliff.

"Flippin' heck, Karen, you didn't expect to, did you? Not really? Just like that? Tell you what,

we'll come back tomorrow. Gus and Richard'll
come like a shot when we tell them what a smashing place it is. Gus can practice his bloomin' mountaineering."

"But . . ." began Karen. Tomorrow might be too
late. She had been so sure she would find the cubs,
but now she began to doubt. The escarpment, after
all, went on for miles. Yet to come so far, and find
the leopard's larder, and then to turn back. She
started to chew her thumbnail and found Jock's hat
still in her hand. She tucked it under her arm,
picked up the top of the water flask and began to
screw it back on.

Jock mopped his face with a grimy handkerchief.
He stuffed it back in his pocket, stood up, and
turned to give Karen his hand. "Come on. Ajax's
waiting." Then:

"Look out!" he shouted, grabbing at her arm.
"Snake!"

Karen dropped the flask as she tumbled forward
on her knees. Seeing nothing, completely bewildered by Jock's sudden action, she twisted round to
grab at the flask as it began to roll away, pulling
her arm away from Jock, and thrusting one leg out
sideways to steady herself.

"Don't be an idiot . . ." she began. Then her foot
slipped as the gravel moved under her heel. She
wobbled, lost her balance, and fell sideways off the
boulder, clutching wildly at Jock as she slid away
from him in a fast-flowing river of stones.

As she fell she screamed.

21

Crash, Rattle, Bang

The sudden noise jolted the cubs out of their fitful sleep.

Rocks and small stones rattled down past their home. Overhead there came a jarring thud, and dirt showered down on the small furry bodies from the roof of the cave. Then a large body crashed heavily onto the ledge below.

Frightened, the cubs shrank together. The dust made its way into their eyes and dry, seeking mouths. They sneezed, wailed unhappily. They were bewildered, miserable, desperately hungry.

Together they set up a twin piercing mew.

22

Something Fierce and Furry

"Karen!"

Jock spread-eagled himself on the lowest boulder, which was now undermined by the landslide and tilted alarmingly. Anchoring himself as best he could by his feet, he wriggled out until he could see as far as was safely possible down the cliff. A haze of dust rose lazily into the air and he could still hear an occasional rock clattering in the depths below him. Above, Ajax was in full cry. There was no sound from Karen.

"Oh corks!" said Jock. "Trust a girl. Hey, Karen —can you hear me? Kaaaaaaaren. KAAAAAAAR-EN!"

His voice, getting shriller as he became more alarmed, echoed back at him mockingly. He called again and again, and Ajax's barks reached a new crescendo.

"Crumbs, oh crumby bloomin' crumbs." Jock stared down the cliff; he gazed up at the top. He tried to wriggle out an extra inch or so, and the boulder moved under him. He heard the crunch and grate of shifting gravel and he froze. When he again dared to breath, he eased himself back off the boulder as gently as he could. Hardly knowing what he was doing, he picked up the empty flask and mechanically replaced the cap. He collected Karen's coat and knapsack and hunted for his hat, and, as he did so, a movement by the side of the rock made him jump. A large lizard slithered from crevice to crevice. Jock stared at it. So that was what he had seen! He had for the moment completely forgotten the "snake" which had started all this trouble.

His hat was missing. It was a treasured possession, and for a moment it seemed desperately important to Jock that he find it. Then mentally he kicked himself. "Jeepers, what does a hat matter? It's Karen," he told himself. He started back up the stony staircase on all fours, helter-skelter, puffing and panting, grazing his bare knees and breaking a fingernail. His one thought now was to get help.

At the top he found Ajax straining at his leash in his anxiety to find out what was going on. His barks changed to eager whines as he saw Jock, who paused by the dog to catch his breath and plan his actions. Rubbing away at Ajax's ears, he recapped. He had a choice. He could climb down the cliff again, taking a different route, and try to find the place where Karen lay, and give her help. But then if she were hurt he might not be able to fetch her back up the cliff by himself. Or he could run now as fast as he could to fetch his brother. Jock was accustomed to turn to Angus for help when he got into hot water. Habit took command. Yes, that must be the best thing to do.

"You stay here, old funny face," he said to Ajax. "It's getting late—gosh, it'll be dark in an hour—and goodness knows what lives around here. If I get lost coming back, your noise will guide us." He remembered the mazelike quality of the bush.

He hugged Ajax fiercely round his black-maned neck, scowled to stop the trembling of his lower lip, and began to thrust his way as quickly as he could down the nearest opening. Ajax bounded forward after him and was brought up short by the leash. Briefly he barked his protests, then flopped down again, his eyes fixed on the still quivering shrubs that marked Jock's passage.

Gradually the sound of snapping twigs and rustling leaves died away. The sun dipped toward the Ngongs, and flocks of small birds began to settle in the trees, gossiping among themselves and squabbling over their favorite perches. The first evening warbler tuned up; he tried a short scale. The creatures of the day were handing over to the creatures of the night.

Ajax laid his chin on his front paws and settled down to wait.

Far down the cliff, on a narrow rock-littered ledge, Karen lay sprawled on her face. She lay still, the sun comforting her shoulder blades. There was gravel in her hair and dust in her mouth and nose. Every bone in her body seemed jarred out of place, and her head throbbed with the beat of a big bass drum. But her ears rang to a different note, a high-pitched squeaking which added to her discomfort and forced her, reluctantly, to move. It would be good to stay quiet, to rest a while, soothed by warmth, if only that nasty noise would stop, thought Karen. I am in bed. I have been dreaming. But everything will soon return to normal if I am allowed to rest in peace.

"I wish you would be quiet," she said out loud.

And realized at once that she was not in bed. Not dreaming. Not at home at all. She opened her gritty eyes, finding her eyelids quite extraordinarily heavy, almost too much for her, and saw dry yellowish dust and shark-gray stone pressed against her cheek.

At that moment there was a sudden rush of air, raising a fresh dust cloud round Karen's head, a swooshing sound, and then a thud which shuddered through the ledge and up into Karen's battered body. Something new had landed on the ledge. Something large.

The throbbing in Karen's head had collected itself in one place on her right temple. She pushed herself up from the rock and, as she raised her head, slowly, warily, to face the newcomer, the throbbing turned to pain, sharp skewers of pain which sent pinpoints of light zigzagging in front of her eyes. Karen groaned and focused her dazzled eyes with difficulty on a shadowy shape a yard away on the ledge. Her nose, lifted from the peppery dust, wrin-

kled as a nauseous smell reached it. She thought of meat, rotten, flyblown meat. The shape hunched toward her, brown wings lifted and obscene neck curved forward. Bright cold eyes met her own. A downward-hooked beak gaped.

She was sharing the ledge with a vulture.

Frightened into rigidity, Karen pressed down against the hard stone as if she hoped to appear part of it. Then fear turned to panic—and panic came to her aid. She screamed, screamed, and scrambled back from the peering vulture which, at her movement, hopped clumsily away from her, hissing, and opening and closing its beak, showing its wormlike tongue and choking Karen with the smell of carrion.

Karen crouched in a niche at the back of the ledge. The pain from her head flooded over her, and she let her head droop forward. Then she caught at her ebbing consciousness and, fumbling round her with her right hand, found a rock and hurled it as hard as she could at the waiting bird of prey.

The rock struck the vulture under its dirty white ruff and the snakelike neck jerked back with the impact. Karen seized another.

"Got you, got you, got you," she triumphed, throwing rocks as fast as she could grab them. She dropped to her knees, tears streaking her mud-patterned face, hurling rocks and yelling at the vulture. Yelling, yelling, yelling, until her dry throat cracked and she stopped, panting, to find the ledge empty. The vulture had flown.

Karen sank back on her heels and leaned her

head against the cliff face. She closed her eyes. For a moment or two she let herself drift into a kind of semi-dream. Then she opened her eyes and sat up. Oddly enough, she felt better. Her arms and legs seemed once more to be part of her, and willing to do what work she asked of them. Her head still pounded, and she explored her forehead with tender fingers. There was an egg-sized lump on her right temple, and stickiness surrounded it. She inspected her fingers and found that the stickiness was blood.

Then she checked over the rest of herself. There was a nasty graze on her left arm, stretching from wrist to elbow, and her watch glass was cracked. She held the watch to her ear; it had stopped. The palms of both hands were scratched as if she had clutched at the rocks as she fell. The knees of her jeans were torn and both knees smarted. There was a purple bruise forming on her left ankle bone. Her body was one big ache.

"But otherwise I feel fine," said Karen loudly, defying the vulture, the cliff and everything else. Her confidence was returning in leaps and bounds. She found her handkerchief and blew her nose. She moistened her lips and longed for water, cold water, rain water, running water. Anything wet.

"Now what do I do?" Karen asked herself. It was a comfort to hear her own voice, and she went on speaking. "I fell down the cliff when Jock yelled 'snake' at me—the clot—and I must have hit this ledge and conked myself on the head. Then that horrid bird turned up and roused me—hey, I wish Jock could have seen me whack him with those stones. He always said I couldn't throw for toffee-apples. Jock—I wonder what happened to Jock?"

She stood up, uncurling gingerly from her cramped position and wincing as she straightened her sore knees. Clutching at an overhanging rock, she peered upwards. There was a cleft above her, filled with a cat's cradle of mud-splattered shrubs and grasses. Farther up she could see a blurred scrape here and there down the cliff face which she guessed might be the path of her fall.

"Jock—Joooooooock!" shouted Karen. And her voice cawed back at her, echoing along the escarpment: "Jock . . . ck . . . ck." Karen listened. There was no answer. Then, faintly, as if from another world, she heard the sound of barking.

"Ajax! Ajax is up there. Good old Ajax." She had forgotten all about him. Why his presence should be so comforting Karen did not bother to work out. If Jock were gone, then surely he had gone for help—always supposing he had not fallen also. This thought struck coldly at Karen. She noticed consciously for the first time the sinking sun and the lengthening shadows. But again the sound of barking carried down to her, and her face brightened.

"That's my boy," said Karen.

"I could just sit here and wait," she went on, chewing at her cuticle and continuing her earlier thought. "But surely—surely Jock is all right and has gone to get help? But what if he isn't—and hasn't? Gosh, I could sit here forever and no one would know." She thought of the oncoming night and the creatures that belonged to that night, and her spine cringed. "Nope, I must try to climb up."

Favoring her left foot, she hobbled along to the right, past the spot where the vulture had sat and inspected her, hoping she was dead. The ledge narrowed and finally disappeared into a slope of loose earth and gravel, impossible to climb.

"That's no good," she said. Back she went to the left, passing the niche, where the ledge was wide enough for her to walk easily. Almost at once she stumbled over something soft. She looked down and grinned. It was Jock's hat. Karen picked it up and twirled it on her finger. "Fancy that," she said. "Of course. I had it when I fell."

A thought came to her, and she peered down. But she was no nearer the bottom of the escarpment than she was the top, and there was no sign of life down there. The game park track was deserted, and the unspoilt Africa she had enthused about to Jock stretched as far as she could see.

She drew her gaze back to her immediate world. At the end of the ledge to the left there was a place which might be climbable. Or would the cleft she had noticed give her a better start?

She crammed Jock's old hat on the back of her head to free her hands and started up. Boy, she was stiff! And climbing hurt her hands. She got one knee up and clutched at a bush, preparing to pull herself onto a flattish rock at the side of the cleft. The bush rustled.

Then, at one and the same time, there came to Karen's nose and ears the smell of carrion and the sound of a small creature crying.

The smell of carrion immediately reminded Karen of the vulture, and she froze where she clung. But the sound also was familiar. She began to recall the squeaking which had so fretted her as she first regained consciousness.

"It wouldn't be vultures—not in there," she said to herself. But she peered around her doubtfully. "What I've got to do is get out of here," she said. "Not bother about mysterious squeakers. It'll be dark before long and for all I know there'll be leopards on the prowl!"

Leopards.

For the first time since her accident she gave a thought to the reason for her presence on the escarpment. Leopards. The leopardess had died—was it only that morning?—and she had come with Jock hunting for orphaned leopard cubs. Because old Mrs. Liversedge had said the escarpment was a likely spot. Leopard cubs. Deserted leopard cubs, crying for mother, crying for food. Squeakers.

"Lord, lordy," breathed Karen, everything else forgotten. "If it is—if it only could be."

Ignoring her cuts and bruises, her pounding head and smarting hands, she hoisted herself onto the rock and pressed the twigs apart. She peered through the leaves. The cleft ran further back than was at first apparent. It narrowed and shrank under a huge slab of rock, overgrown and camouflaged,

turning out of sight to the left, becoming a cave. A
lair.

The plaintive mewing grew louder. Karen
crouched down and struggled through the bush.

"Here—kitty, kitty, kitty. Here, kitty," she said
idiotically. She clucked and cooed, and made all the
soothing noises she could think of, all the time
pressing further into the dim recess. Things long
and slender rolled from under her groping hand,
and she looked down and found herself kneeling
among small bones and balls of grayish-yellow fluff
which smelled unpleasantly. But the carrion smell
was all about her, and another smell, musty and
acrid—the smell of the lion house at the zoo.

"I must be bonkers," she thought suddenly.
"Here I am, miles from nowhere, all alone, crawling into a leopard's lair. What if the leopard's at
home?" Did she hear an echo of her mother's voice:
"Karen, are you being sensible?"

But she struggled on. She was convinced that
she had reached the end of her quest. Indeed, when
ahead of her a shape appeared, a tiny brownish
shape dimly spotted, which opened a tiny mouth
and mewed a mew not so tiny at all, she was not
surprised.

"Oh, the little thing," said Karen. "The baby
furry thing."

She reached for the cub, which wobbled away
from her, tiny ears laid back against the rounded
head, frail back arching, wild baby eyes narrowing.
The cub mewed and spat.

"Something fierce and furry!" breathed Karen.

23

Rescue

As Karen reached for the first cub the second tumbled into sight. Karen drew back her hand, content for the moment to watch the two as they collided and subsided together in a mound of mottled fluff.

"What a bundle," she said fondly. "Any more of you in there?" But nothing else emerged from the lair.

The cubs seemed soothed by the contact of their bodies and the mewing died away; but when Karen moved, trying to settle herself more comfortably half in, half out, of the spiky branches, two kitten faces turned toward her and two pink triangular mouths opened, letting out such a piercing wail that Karen's hands flew momentarily to her ears.

Again she reached a hand toward them and this

time was able to smooth the silky fur on one rounded head before the cub shrank away, while the second cub bumped its dry nose accidentally against her fingers and immediately began to suck. It tickled. Karen giggled.

"Perhaps I smell of earth," she thought. "And not of people. And I must look about the right size for a mother thing, down on all fours like this."

But even if they would let her pick them up, how could she carry them? She would need her hands for the climb in front of her.

Should she leave them, marking the spot as best she could, and come back next day to rescue them, bringing help? They looked so small, so pathetically small and lost, tumbled there in front of her. Karen remembered the vulture. And there were so many predators, large and small, constantly on the hunt for the weak and unwary. If the cubs strayed from the lair they would not live long. No, they must go with her, that was plain.

If only she had her jacket. But that, presumably, still lay on a boulder high on the cliff. She could tuck them inside her shirt, hoping the warmth of her body would lull them to sleep. But she remembered the story of the Spartan boy and the fox. She was battered enough already. Karen scratched her head, wondering what was best. And then she remembered. Jock's hat!

It was gone from her head but it could not be far. She wriggled backwards away from the clutching twig fingers of the bush and felt oddly flattered as a new crescendo of squeaks broke out behind her.

"They miss me!" she said, and giggled again.

There was the hat, just outside the bushes. Clinging to a rock with one hand, she picked it up and banged it against the cliff face to remove some of the dried mud decorating it. Opened out it made quite a big bag.

Back she crawled, careless of aches and pains, and found the cubs where she had left them, huddled together. They drew back as she came crackling through the bush, both baby noses wrinkling up in identical snarl creases. Their whiskers were already luxuriant.

Karen looked at them lovingly and spoke in a voice which she tried to make calm, firm and reassuring, all at once, the way her mother spoke to Jenny. "Now then, babies, come to mother," she said. "Here we go. One at a time." She slid her hand under one warm, feather-light body and lifted the cub. Very gently she slid the squirming baby into the crown of the hat. It hooked itself to the brim with its bent-pin claws and squawled its indignation at her. A moment more, and both cubs looked at her from their new nest, eyes owllike with astonishment. She shook the hat a little, easing out the claws that caught in the felt, and the cubs bunched together in the crown looking, she thought, surprisingly snug.

Karen sat back on her heels and looked at the cubs, her own eyes bright with pleasure. She had found them. She had them safe. She was still a long way from home and night was falling, but this seemed of minor importance. She, Karen Elliott, had found the leopard cubs.

The thought did slide through her mind that perhaps these were not the orphaned cubs, that perhaps at that moment an irate leopard mother might be hurtling toward her. But she dismissed the thought. It didn't fit the picture. "It was Fate," said Karen. "With a capital 'F.' I was meant to find them."

But now she had to get out of there as fast as she could. Free once more from the embraces of the bush, she stood up, holding the hat by the opposing sides of the brim. Slumped at the bottom, the cubs seemed to be settling to sleep. She began to climb.

A long step brought her onto the protruding slab of rock which made the roof of the lair. Then there came a scramble up jagged rocks harsh to her scraped hands. Then she reached another ledge, small and grassy, which she guessed from the scattered droppings and nearby holes to be the front yard of a colony of rocky hyraxes. She sat for a moment on the close-cropped turf, catching her breath, and peeped in at her precious bundle. One little face peered back at her; the smoky eyes shone in the growing dusk. The second cub slept, chin nestling on its sister's neck, dreamily sucking fur.

Karen glanced westward. Long shadow fingers reached toward her from the hills as the sun sank behind them. She stood up, straightened her back with an effort, and looked about her for the next step. A sound drew her gaze upward.

Out from the top of the escarpment flew the two crowned cranes, heavy wings threshing the air, the rocks ringing with their deep trumpeting call. They dipped toward the plains, and Karen's heart went winging with them as her eyes followed their strange elongated silhouettes.

She sighed, and brought her mind back to the job on hand. The next few minutes she spent breathlessly feeling for toeholds and clinging to spurs of rock and tufts of grass which fortunately stayed anchored to their scanty pockets of soil. She found time to think that it might be useful to have fingernails.

Then came a check. Facing her on one side was a slide of murram, while on the other the cliff went sharply up. She chose the murram. Treading sidewards she worked her way up the slope, every step an effort. The gravel stirred uneasily beneath her feet. She was nearly to the top when she slipped.

Karen sat down and dug in her heels as the gravel gathered momentum round her. She tobogganed three yards on the seat of her jeans before she was able to halt herself, hampered as she was by the need to protect the cubs. The dirt settled everywhere, in eyes, ears, nostrils, mouth. She sneezed and choked and felt tears prick her eyes. She longed to give up, to sit back and howl her eyes out. Better still, to stamp her feet and scream her rage at the world. But there was no one to hear her, so: "Poof!" said Karen, clutching her precious bundle.

Slowly, with infinite care, she struggled up the slope once more, step by wary step. Her legs trembled and her back ached from concentration as well as bruises by the time she scrambled onto a solidly based boulder where she was able to rest.

But she felt proud. She looked back at the conquered slope and laughed out loud, a croak of a laugh, but a laugh. She longed desperately for something to drink. The bump on her forehead was throbbing more intrusively, as if something inside her head sought a way out.

"Gosh, I wonder how long it's been since I fell?" Her watch was broken. "Surely old Jock could have got to Timbuktu and back again by now?" She guessed she had been unconscious for a brief time only, though she must have lain still enough and long enough to encourage the vulture.

She turned wearily and clambered on. At least she could make out the edge of the cliff now. There was not so much further to go, and the boulders made stepping stones; but directly above her the cliff overhung, and she began to edge to the right. A thought struck her, and she began to call.

"Ajax. Aaaaajax!" She whistled as shrilly as she could through sticky lips. And instantly there came the intensely welcome sound, the warm, cosy, *beautiful* sound, of Ajax barking. "Good boy!" yelled Karen. I'll never never tell him to shut up again, she vowed to herself. On she plodded, changing Jock's hat from hand to hand. It was far heavier, she thought, than it had been to begin with.

"They must be growing," thought Karen, proudly and absurd. "My cubs!"

She could see the tops of trees and the smother of

bush in those places where it grew to the brink. She increased her pace, ignoring the weariness that weighed her down more heavily than her bundle. Up she went, scrabbling on hands and knees over dimly seen rocks which crouched in the gloom as if ready to spring. All that was left of the sun was an orange afterglow haloing the hills and deepening the shadows to black. The cubs, bounced and bumped in the rough-and-tumble journey, began to mew once more, and Karen cradled the hat closely against her body to spare them as much jolting as possible. The top. She was nearly at the top. Everything would be all right once she reached the top.

She pulled herself triumphantly up the last stretch, her hands clutching the cliff's grassy fringe and, once over the rim, rested on one knee and lowered the hat to the ground. She had made it. She let out a huge sigh of relief. It was hard to tell just where she was. She waited a moment, breathing hard and peering around her. Then she began to call again, happily, to Ajax, whose barks had suddenly ceased. Once she found him she would be orientated.

"Ajax? Old Dogface? Where are you, boy?"

But the sound that answered her was not a bark but a hideous cackle, a goblin whoop and wail that froze Karen where she kneeled and left her straining her eyes toward the trees, face blanched and mouth gaping.

Almost simultanously she heard Ajax growl his deep ferocious growl, the growl that sent strangers leaping for the house or calling for help but which had never, to her knowledge, been followed by anything fiercer than a tail wag.

It was typical of Karen that, even as she cowered at the cliff edge as terrified as she had ever been in her whole life, her thought was for Ajax, not herself—gormless Ajax who had grown big but not up, and still needed her for protection. She had left him tied to a tree, vulnerable, helpless before attack.

Yelling had helped with the vulture. Karen yelled now, with all her remaining strength, and waved her arms, though her tired muscles screamed protest.

She could make out the hyenas, two of them, skulking in and out at the edge of the trees, their misshapen shadows leaping like evil spirits in the fiery half light. Whether their attention had been on Ajax when she disturbed them, or whether they had just arrived she did not know, but now they turned their blunt muzzles from dog to girl and back, not brave enough to close in, nor yet scared enough to make off without further investigation. Karen had time to think of the alternatives facing her; of trying to fight her way home with dog and cubs through scrub and thorn trees, or of remaining alone at the cliff edge in the growing dark, awaiting help, with the hyenas edging nearer and nearer. Her heart shriveled inside her.

But she kept on yelling. And Ajax barked furiously, straining at the leash and thrashing about as he tried to free himself.

It flashed through Karen's mind that she might

be wise to climb back down the cliff a little way, but this meant abandoning Ajax—and it was escape back into the trap she had left. Instead she began to shuffle forward a little, away from the rim of the cliff, which was dangerously close. If she could work her way along toward Ajax. . . .

She moved awkwardly, still in a kneeling position, not daring to take her eyes off the hyenas. A rock ground painfully into her right knee and she overbalanced, dropping one hand to the turf ahead of her. Small feet stumbled over her fingers, and she snatched up her hands with a fresh yell which was more of a squeal. Rats?

It was then that she remembered the cubs, and looked over her shoulder for Jock's hat which she had dumped at the cliff edge. She could see its lumpy black outline. A wobbling black outline. She swung about and grabbed for it, twisting back immediately to face the hyenas. Only one little form took shape under her searching fingers and she glanced around in panic, sifting the gloom with desperate eyes, seeking the missing cub somewhere between herself and the lurking hyenas.

It was there!

She saw the small blurred shadow move and stop, fumble on, and flop again; and she saw, also, one of

the hyenas leave the protection of the trees and come snuffling toward the runaway cub.

Lurching to her feet, Karen sprang forward, giving at the same time the loudest scream she had yet managed. And, as she did so, Ajax also leaped.

There was a sharp *crack,* the slap of racing feet, a growing growling rumble, and Ajax, ablaze with reckless courage, tore to Karen's aid. Unable to stop, he hit the barrellike rib cage of the hyena, battering-ram hard.

Karen snatched up the cub and shrank back as far as she dared. Helpless and afraid, she watched her champion prepare to do battle.

The surprise of his attack gave Ajax his main advantage. Big he was, and brave he was. But he was no match for a pair of hyenas whose jaws were made for cracking bones discarded by lions. The hyena was knocked off its feet, and Ajax tumbled over the struggling body. Both animals rolled over, snapping and snarling at nothing. Both animals recovered themselves, and the hyena wheeled on the dog with wickedly grinning jaws, ready to snap like a bear trap through muscle and bone. The two animals, necks bristling, circled stiff-legged around each other, shaking the earth with their snarls. The second hyena snickered nervously and slunk to the right, ready to take Ajax from the rear.

Karen screamed again.

As the noise of her own scream faded, over the snarls, growls and wails, a new sound reached Karen's ears. The sound of shouting. Then out of the trees burst Mungai, startling in his white Salvation Army uniform, his panga in one hand and a lantern in the other. Close at his heels came Richard, Angus and Jock.

The hyenas turned tail and fled. Ajax swaggered a few steps after them, barking his contempt, then he turned and pranced back to protect the group behind him. He had come of age.

The boys crowded round Karen, their torches dramatically spotlighting her mud-and-blood-streaked face. She stood with one leopard cub clinging to her shoulder and the other nestled between her hands. It was Karen's proudest moment, and it almost made up for the trials of the day.

"I ran all the way," said Jock, panting to prove it.

"Are you OK? We came as quick as we could," said Richard and Angus both together.

"Eh jambo, Missy," said Mungai, as if nothing unusual had happened. *"Habari?"*

There was a pause. Karen looked at Mungai, an avenging angel in the glory of his white uniform. At Richard, handsome and big-brotherly. At Angus, who had his mountain-climbing rope slung in a roll over his shoulders and wasn't so bad really. And at Jock. Clumsy old Jock. Jock the substitute who turned up trumps. Jock, his forehead gleaming with sweat and his eyes glowing with admiration.

She loved them all.

24

Wish Come True

Karen remembered very little of the journey home. Her rescuers, it turned out, had come by road on bicycles instead of crossing the golf course. Jock had perched on the crossbar of Mungai's, and Richard and Angus had shared Kukombe's venerable model. Once out of the mazelike scrub and across the plantation, Karen was wheeled home by Mungai, with Richard to hold her in the saddle; for, by that time, she was reeling from side to side with exhaustion. Angus wheeled the other bike, Jock was allowed to carry the cubs as it was his hat, and Ajax led the procession.

At the back of her weary mind, ever since she had discovered the cubs, had been the thought of her mother's reception of them. Would she exclaim in dismay? Shriek with horror? At last put her foot down? Karen need not have worried. Mrs. Elliott did exclaim in dismay when she first set eyes on Karen and heard a garbled explanation from the boys; but her reaction to the cubs was much the same as Karen's own.

"Oh, the little things!" said Mrs. Elliott. "The poor wee babies."

Her next comment was more practical. "Mrs. Liversedge—she's just the person. Richard, gallop away on your long legs and bring her back with you. She'll take care of the leopard cubs and I'll take care of my girl cub."

She got down to work. Karen was half ushered, half carried into the bathroom, where she was undressed, bathed, and medicated, without herself having to lift a finger.

By that time sleep was washing over her in dizzying waves. But although she meekly drank the hot milk her mother insisted on, and eyed her soft bed longingly, she then turned stubborn.

"You must let me see them. I won't go to bed till I've seen them," she said. And she was swaddled in her dressing gown and escorted to the dining room where the cubs were the center of attention. Mrs. Liversedge was feeding one cub with a fountain-pen filler while Angus (Angus!) was feeding the second with one of Jenny's old bottles. Karen had time to notice that Angus had lost his supercilious expression and looked young and eager; for the first time she saw a resemblance between the brothers.

But then they realized she was there, and her reception overwhelmed her. Richard seated her ten-

derly in the chair at the head of the table and
Jock fussed round her with cushions. Angus, without being asked, handed over his baby and bottle
to Karen. This she appreciated very much; but,
when she found the bottle blurring before her eyes,
she passed them back to him.

"You do it, Angus," she said. "I'll have my turn
tomorrow."

"There's a boy cub and a girl, Karen," said Richard, his face alive with interest. "And the boy is
much bigger and stronger than the girl—he's the
one taking the bottle. She couldn't manage the
nipple so Mrs. Liversedge is squirting her."

"Is she all right?" Karen turned anxiously to
Mrs. Liversedge.

"Oh, she'll do, my dear. Don't worry. She's a
good little gel," said Mrs. Liversedge, replenishing
the filler and disregarding the milky splashes down
her jacket.

"Now, Karen." Her mother was standing over
her.

"All right, Mummy, I'll come."

She got to her feet and staggered as her legs
melted beneath her. Jock and Richard leaped to
her aid.

She smiled at them both, her face lopsided under
the strappings on her forehead. She had the begin-
nings of a magnificent black eye. Then her mother
led her away.

But Karen had one more thing to say. As she
reached the door she turned back.

"Mrs. Liversedge?" she said. The lined old face

bent so intently over the wriggling cub turned toward her.

"The younger generation did its best," said Karen. And went contentedly to bed.

There were three stories to match up next day. To an audience which hung on her every word, Karen told of her encounter with the vulture, the finding of the cubs, her scramble up the cliff, and, finally, the meeting with the hyenas and Ajax's bravery in coming to her rescue.

"Corks," said Jock. "And I missed it! I knew I should've stayed. But I was scared of starting a bloomin' rock slide right down on top of you."

He had hurried the best he could through the stretch of country he and Karen now called the wilderness. But he had lost himself and could only guess that he had gone round in circles for a while. When he finally reached the road he had been lucky enough to meet the Vicar zooming along in his Mini-Minor and had been given a lift up to the Langata Road.

"Yes, you *mjinga*," said Angus, pulling Jock's nose. "You mutton-headed nincompoop. Why you didn't ask him for help I still can't imagine."

"But this was a secular matter," said Jock primly. "I didn't want to bother him." To tell the truth there had been only one thought in his head, and that was to find his brother, the natural person to get him out of scrapes.

Then Richard took the story over. Jock had come, puffing and blowing like a sounding whale, into the Faulkners' garden, and it had been some minutes before he could tell a coherent story. Richard had then raced to find his father, but Mr. Faulkner was out and so, they soon found, was Mr. Elliott. (Both fathers, it turned out, had slipped away to play golf that afternoon and were in the clubhouse quietly enjoying their beer all the while the commotion was going on.)

The boys had not wanted to bother Mrs. Elliott, who was busy bathing Jenny, so they had planned to start off by themselves. But on the drive they had met Mungai, returning from his meeting, and he had taken charge. They had borrowed Kukombe's bicycle and made as much speed as possible.

"But," concluded Richard. "If ever there was a naaaaasty moment, it was trekking through that scrub and hearing, first the hyenas laughing their heads off, then old Ajax giving tongue, and then you, shrieking like a banshee! Phew!"

"But at least the row guided us to you," said Angus. "Jock hadn't a clue which way to go. Mungai had a pretty good idea, though. He says he used to go hunting round that way when he was a boy— and it was always a leopardy spot."

"Sometimes I think I should keep you in a baby harness, like Jenny," said Mrs. Elliott to Karen. "Whatever will you be up to next?"

"Would you like me to sit at home and sew a fine seam?" asked Karen.

"It would make a very pleasant change," said her mother grimly. "You can start by mending the knees of your jeans!"

But there was more important work to be done. The half-starved cubs needed constant attention, night and day, and small frequent feeds were necessary until the right milk mixture and acceptable quantity were found by experiment. For the first few days, in fact, everyone willing was roped in to take turns at the incessant feeding that went on.

Karen's own recovery was quick enough and complete enough to ensure her return to school on Monday, the first day of the summer term—much to her disgust. Although she could not help being flattered by the interest her black eye, and her story, aroused, she felt she was needed at home. But by then someone new had taken a hand at cub-rearing. Tina.

Mrs. Elliott had a story to tell about this. The very first night, while Karen slept the deep sleep of exhaustion, her mother had struggled to settle the cubs in a nest of old blankets warmed by a hot-water bottle; but, every time she moved away, the cubs straggled after her. She had finally corralled them in a large box, but they had cried the night through. She had been wary of the dogs' possible reaction to the cubs and had shut them out of harm's way. On the Sunday evening, however, Tina had eased her way in through a half-latched door and the first thing Mrs. Elliott knew about it was when Tina picked up a mewling cub by the scruff of its neck and returned it to the blankets. Then, with a grunt and a sigh, she settled herself down with them and proceeded to lick them into a state of blissful subjection.

"And a good thing too," said Richard wisely. "Cubs reared by hand get all sorts of things wrong with their insides because they don't get the massaging from their baby-minders that they do from the wild old Mums. A licking a day keeps the vet away, you know."

"Oh you—you clever stick, you," said Karen. "Anyone would think you'd brought up dozens of 'em."

In fact they had all turned into experts on leopard-cub rearing. Theories bred like maggots in cheese. Tina was Head Nurse. Karen was Official Parent. Mrs. Liversedge was Adviser-in-Chief. Mrs. Elliott was Head Cook and Bottle Washer. And the menfolk had feeding privileges. At their earnest plea, Angus and Jock stayed on for another month at the Faulkners'. Telegrams were sent, followed by letters. Hasty answers were received, and, by special arrangement with the school, the Duncans came and went each day with Richard.

"Well, leopard cubs don't turn up every day," said Jock. "It's bloomin' educational!"

"Indubitably," said Angus. And he grinned.

Despite all this, the cubs thrived. Their bellies plumped out, their coats became soft and glossy, and they soon began to recognize their adoptive parents. Once an acceptable formula had been found for them, and regular feeding times established, peace ("Of a sort," said Mrs. Elliott) returned to the Elliott household. The first few days were the most difficult.

By the end of May, however, the cubs could lap

from a saucer, which made things much easier, and rice and cod-liver oil were added to their milk. They were then thought to be about six or seven weeks old. The rains, which had been dribbling on, ceased altogether, and it was possible for them to spend most days out of doors in the old puppy house under the jacaranda tree. A new wire fence, three times as high, was built completely surrounding the tree.

Karen kept careful notes of the cubs' behavior. It had occurred to her that, though she could not grow up to be a game warden, she could be a naturalist or a zoologist. So she was practicing.

The male cub remained the more powerful and forceful of the pair. He soon began to play and loved a rough and tumble with the boys. He tried his claws and teeth on everything that came his way. He had come to be called the conventional Swahili name of Chui, but the spelling was soon changed to "Chewey."

The female was Karen's favorite. She named her Moshi, the Swahili word for smoke, because of the soft swirling shade of her changing eyes during the first few weeks. Moshi took longer to regain her strength than did her brother, and her nature was more affectionate and gentle. Karen sat, in the early weeks, and cuddled her for hours, her wish at last come true, her fierce and furry pet asleep on her knee.

For Moshi could change in a twinkling from docile kitten to spitfire. She would race round the room with wicked ears and the wind in her tail, assault the curtains, and claw the carpet. Or fly up Karen's trousered legs, the weight tugging at her waistband, every inch a pinprick. Moshi's eyes would narrow to glinting golden slits and her fur would bristle like a thistle. Karen loved her dearly.

By July the cubs were eating meat. They were expert tree climbers and so big and husky that it became necessary to cut their claws so that they would not accidentally hurt Tina, still their constant companion. Ajax looked down his nose at them; but then, he was very dignified these days.

It had been agreed from the first that the cubs would stay with Karen until they were six months old. Then they would leave, at first to go to the animal orphanage run by the Nairobi Game Park. There Karen would still be able to visit them and play with them. Later, possibly, they would go to zoos. Karen accepted this without fuss. She remembered Richard talking about the upsets caused by fully grown pet lions and she knew there had been very few cases of completely domesticated leopards, even if her parents had been willing and able to afford the cost of keeping one in food. She had learned already that Chewey was unpredictable, and would greet her with affection one day and suspicion the next. She now handled him with gloves.

As the cubs changed, it sometimes seemed to her friends that Karen changed also. She grew gentler, more thoughtful, more patient, yet also more self-reliant. She paid frequent visits to Mrs. Liversedge (who had somehow become Aunt Kate), to ask her advice or just talk about Kenya, and an odd friendship struck up between the old Africa-lover and the young.

She was good friends with all three boys and played no favorites, and they haunted her house as once she had haunted theirs.

"She's growing up," said her mother to her father, and sighed. But there was still Jenny to fuss over, to guide and teach and rescue from peril; still someone whose problems were caused by honey and doorknobs, puddles and going downstairs.

One day toward the end of July Karen sat in her garden, nursing Moshi and talking to Richard. Tina lay by her side and Ajax sat, a dignified adult male, guarding them from under the moonflower tree. Karen had had a visitor that afternoon, a reporter taking photographs and wanting a story for an American magazine. Karen had become used to publicity on a small scale. Her rescue of the cubs and the climb up the escarpment had been written up by the Nairobi newspapers. This was the first time, however, that her fame had threatened to spread further afield.

"What fun if Granny saw the photos in England," she said, smoothing Moshi's silky coat. She looked at the cub admiringly. "She's going to grow up just like her mother. Just plain beautiful. But it's strange, isn't it, and sad too, that I only have her because her mother died? I mean, I love having her, it's what I always wanted. She's like a mixture of Honey Bear and the leopardess. But I never would have wished my wish if I'd realized it could only come true through a tragedy. But that must always be the case, mustn't it? You don't take a lion cub, or leopard, away from a living mother! And one wild free animal is worth a hundred pets.

"Granny had a pet saying," continued Karen. "It went like this: 'Take care on what you set your heart, for it will surely come to pass.' I used not to know what she meant, but now I do. Old people are right sometimes."

"What will you do with the cubs when you go to Mombasa?" asked Richard. The summer holidays loomed ahead and Richard and Karen were looking forward to a trip to the sea, where they would swim in tropical-warm waters, hunt for shells, and go goggle fishing over the coral reefs.

"Aunt Kate has offered to take them. She's a duck," said Karen fondly. "Mummy says she's kind to me because she sympathizes with girls in this world. Aunt Kate had five brothers and four sons— and her husband hunted elephants for fun! Cow elephants, I bet."

"How's Bruin getting on these days? I must go and visit him."

"Dogo rules him with a rod of iron. Bruin has the bulk, but Dogo has the brain!" And Karen laughed and turned her face to the sun. It was a rare sunny day, not typical of the cold season, when day after day passed cool and overcast. "Jock says next time Tina has pups he's pretty sure his mother will let him have one."

Jock and Angus were back at home, since their parents had returned from Scotland at the end of

June, but they came often on visits; and Jock wrote lively, ungrammatical letters to Karen. His old felt hat was now enshrined in a glass case.

"And Angus is going to let me come mountaineering when you go in the holidays."

"Good old Gus." Richard watched Ajax march majestically across the lawn and stand staring up at the veranda, head on one side. "What's Ajax up to?"

"It's Oswald. He can't make him out. Oswald sits up there some afternoons and Ajax always stares at him." Oswald, a newcomer to the Elliott household, was a small speckled barn owl. He had been attracted, not by the honey, but by the rats in the roof, and the pattering overhead was giving way to squeaks and hoots and snores. Mrs. Elliott approved of Oswald.

"We run an animal hotel," said Karen. "All modern conveniences. Homes provided for bees, rats and owls. Food laid on."

(There was a humming in the air, a distant throbbing that vibrated in their ears. Ajax turned round and stared at the sky. Tina shook her head till her ears flapped. Moshi opened one eye and Chewey climbed the jacaranda tree.)

"Remember?" went on Karen. "Remember how miserable I was when the puppies went? I thought nothing nice was ever going to happen again. But things did. Look at us now—we have leopards on the lawn, rats in the roof, owls under the eaves. There's a dormouse in the radio. . . ." She stopped short. The humming sound had grown in volume until it canceled conversation. They all stared upwards.

Down from the trees, like a genie emerging from a bottle, spiraling, twisting, zigging and zagging, came a cloud of black smoke. It zoomed. It hummed. It buzzed.

It swept across the garden and turned itself into a swarm of wild bees. They made for the veranda and clustered around a rain pipe.

"As I was saying," finished Karen, hugely delighted. "There's a dormouse in the radio—and bees round the rain pipe. That's Africa for you." She paused, and looked dreamily down at the cub on her lap.

"There's just one thing left unfinished. We'll never know what became of the other leopard. I wonder. . . ."

25

My Lord Leopard

The male leopard, stretched to his full lordly length, sprawled on a sunlit tongue of rock sticking out over the gorge. His wounds had long since healed, though scars still showed, stripes among the rosettes on his coat. His ears were notched like a felon's. One eyelid drooped, the muscle weakened by the deep festering bite of the dog baboon, but his eyes glowed cool and green and dangerous. He looked what he was, the veteran of many battles, a tough, a killer.

He panted open-mouthed, hot, enjoying the heat, easing heavy shoulders, relaxing steel-sinewed legs.

On the far side of the gorge the cliffs rose less high. He could see the plains, yellowing now as the memory of the rains receded and the grasses ripened. There the grass-eaters moved steadily across

his line of vision, nibbling as they went, as if pulled by invisible strings—konkoni, wildebeest, zebra, impala, Grant's and Thomson's gazelles. Giraffe arranged themselves against the horizon, photogenic, elegant. Warthogs jerked forward on their knees. Ostriches paraded, military style.

There came the beat of powerful wings, and the

thick neck arched as the leopard twisted his head to follow the downward rush of a tawny eagle after hyrax. He watched the movements below him, storing the information away: a herd of reedbuck emerging from cover and hesitating as the eagle's shadow skimmed them; bat-eared foxes nose-diving into their burrows; two crowned cranes calmly winging their way toward a water hole.

A baboon barked a warning. A monkey chattered with fright. A pied crow gave a hostile croak.

The tawny eagle missed his prey and screamed his rage. The noise panicked a flock of francolin across an open stretch of grass. The eagle swooped again—and rose, successful, a plump speckled form tight in his talons. The leopard licked his lips, saliva pooling in his mouth. In his mind a picture formed, a taste returned. Feathers, soft flesh, warm blood. He came to his feet in a single boneless surge. And turned and stared along the gorge. And then beyond again.

He moved his paws, kneading the rock beneath him. His tail switched from side to side, and he paced the rock restlessly. The gorge had been his home for some months. He had lived well. But all at once he felt the need to travel, to revisit old stamping grounds, walk old boundaries.

Soon he would be on the move, out of the park, matching his wits once more with man—and woe betide the poultry farms.

For there is no way to fence a leopard.

That's Africa for you.

29712